THE
DESERT PRINCE'S
PROPOSAL

THE DESERT PRINCE'S PROPOSAL

BY

NICOLA MARSH

MILLS & BOON®
Pure reading pleasure™

First published in Great Britain 2008
Large Print edition 2008
Harlequin Mills & Boon Limited,
Eton House, 18-24 Paradise Road, 20183352
Richmond, Surrey TW9 1SR

© Nicola Marsh 2008

ISBN: 978 0 263 20096 6

Set in Times Roman 17 on 21 pt.
16-1108-40490

Printed and bound in Great Britain
by CPI Antony Rowe, Chippenham, Wiltshire

For my very special Nan,
who takes great pride in every book I write
(and who introduced me to the wonderful world of
Mills & Boon all those years ago!).

CHAPTER ONE

'I AM NOT getting into that thing!'

Bria Green glared at the chauffeur, who stared at her with amused detachment like he'd seen it all before, and pointed at the gleaming-black limo parked at the kerb.

'I didn't ask to be picked up. Who sent you?'

The chauffeur, simply known as 'Len', from his name tag, removed his cap and rubbed at a shiny dome almost as highly polished as his car.

'Look, miss. I'm just doing my job. Your name and flight details were on my list, so here I am. I don't know who makes the bookings, I just follow instructions.'

Bria's anger deflated a tad. It wasn't this

guy's fault that Daddy dearest was up to his old tricks again.

'Miss?'

Len held open the door to the limo, and she wavered slightly before a strong waft of spanking-new leather and wood polish hit her like a frigid gust on an icy Melbourne day.

She hated the smell: rich, pungent, nauseating. The smell she'd grown to hate as a child when she'd been dropped off at the school gates every morning, and had faced the merciless teasing of the other kids for turning up to school in a chauffeured limo.

Shaking her head, she backed away from the open door like an abseiler having second thoughts about jumping off a cliff.

'No. I can't. I'm sorry.'

Len frowned, staring at her with genuine confusion in his crinkly brown eyes.

'But, miss, I'm instructed to take you to the Mansion hotel. It's my employer's orders.'

Taking a deep breath, she clutched her suitcase handle, gripped by an irrational fear that if she released it for one second it would be whisked away and stuffed into the limo's boot, leaving her no choice but to enter the opulent confines of the car.

'Excuse me, is there a problem here? Do you need some help?'

Great, just what she needed, some stranger with an upper-class accent poking his nose into her business.

With her temper rising by the minute, she forced a tight smile and looked up at the man, determined to fob him off, ditch Len and find the nearest taxi to take her to the hotel.

However, the first part of her plan faltered when her wary gaze met curious dark-brown eyes, eyes she would've flicked past if they weren't part of a striking ensemble of high cheekbones, strong jaw, straight Roman nose, Mediterranean tan and black-as-coal hair which framed his face, highlighting the perfection.

Striking? Who was she kidding? The guy was gorgeous, imposing, and staring at her with obvious concern.

'I'm fine,' she said, waving him away with one hand while maintaining a death grip on her suitcase.

She travelled extensively to promote Motive, her architectural business. She knew the dangers of landing in a strange city and being accosted by wackos, no matter how incredible they looked.

'You sure?'

His deep voice rippled over her, the posh accent reminiscent of the time she'd spent in London. The time she'd rather forget.

'Positive.'

She nodded emphatically and turned away, only to be confronted by the burgundy leather seats of the limo, and a bar tucked discreetly into the far door.

Suddenly, the choice between getting into

the limo and possibly being abducted didn't seem so far apart after all.

'I'm sorry for intruding, but it appears you don't want to get into the limousine with this man.'

Len puffed up like a jellyfish.

'Hey! I resent what you're implying, sir. I'm only doing my job, and right now that's taking Miss Green to her hotel.'

The stranger ignored Len and focussed that unnerving, steady gaze on her.

'Would you prefer to take a taxi?'

'Yes, please.'

She nodded, grateful that someone had picked up on her distress and wasn't making a big deal about it.

All she wanted to do was grab a cab to the hotel, take a long, hot bath and prepare for her presentation. She didn't need any more dramas.

'Miss Green, are you sure?'

Len didn't give up easily, and she managed a weary smile to reassure him.

'I'm sure. And don't worry about your employer. If you have any problems, get them to contact me direct.'

Shrugging, Len doffed his cap in her direction before closing the door and heading to the driver's side of the car, obviously washing his hands of the crazy lady who'd rather ride in a beat-up taxi than a stretch limo.

'Thank you,' she said, turning to the stranger, but already looking past him, her eager gaze fixed on the last taxi standing at the rank.

'My pleasure. Would you care to share my taxi?'

'Your taxi?'

She knew it. Mr Nice Guy had an ulterior motive. He'd helped her get rid of Len only to coerce her into goodness knew what during what could prove an interminable taxi ride to anywhere.

An amused gleam lit his dark eyes, as if he could read her suspicious mind.

'I took the liberty of snaring the last taxi for myself. The driver said a major football match has just finished in the city, so there won't be another taxi along for a while.'

'That's okay. I'll take the shuttle bus.'

Though that would put her plans of having a bath and time to prepare her talk way behind, considering she was staying at Werribee, miles out of town.

He hesitated for a moment before shrugging.

'Suit yourself. I'm staying at the Mansion hotel, and you probably would've been out of my way.'

'You're staying at the Mansion? Are you there for the architects' conference too?'

'No, I'm not attending the conference. I'm into property development, and have other business to attend to while I'm there.'

Bria toyed with the leather handle on her

case as she weighed up her options: take a ride with a handsome stranger to her hotel in the relative comfort of a taxi, or spend an interminable few hours while the shuttle stopped at countless hotels.

She may be stubborn, as her father repeatedly told her, but she wasn't stupid, and the decision was a no-brainer.

Sticking out her hand, she said, 'Sorry for being a bit abrupt. I'm Bria Green, and if your offer for a ride still stands I'd like to take you up on it. Strange coincidence, but I'm staying at the Mansion too.'

He raised a dark eyebrow as he clasped her hand in his.

'Sam Wali. And of course you can share the taxi with me.'

'Great.'

She smiled, a strange flutter of uncertainty causing her to leave her hand in his longer than necessary. His hand was warm, his grip firm without crushing, and though she didn't sense anything untoward from him a slight shiver skittered down her spine at the intensity of his dark stare.

'Do you believe in fate, Miss Green?'

Bria dropped her hand quickly, hoping she hadn't given him the wrong idea, and wondering how she got herself into these situations. For a strong, opinionated career-woman, she had a habit of making the odd impulsive decision which had far-reaching repercussions.

Clearing her throat, she said, 'I believe we make our own fate, Mr Wali.'

He smiled, and all her misgivings disappeared in an instant, the genuine warmth lighting his face and capturing her with its animation.

'Please call me Sam. After all, we're going to be sharing a taxi together.'

'Bria,' she said, hating the flicker of awareness his simple words elicited—the flicker that told her, no matter how strongly she'd sworn off men after Ellis 'the lowlife' Finley, this handsome stranger had the power to intrigue her. 'And thanks, once again.'

He barely acknowledged her gratitude.

'You are ready to depart?'

She nodded, biting back a grin at his formal speech patterns. Combined with a strong upper-class English accent, a designer suit which appeared hand-made to fit his imposing physique, and the solid platinum-and-gold watch on his left wrist, Sam exuded wealth and power—everything in a guy that usually made her wary, yet she found herself nodding anyway.

'Come. We will go.'

Before she could move, he'd whisked her suitcase away and was heading to the waiting taxi, his long strides eating up the footpath.

Hoping she was doing the right thing, and too tired to care one way or the other, she followed him, taking the time to admire the flattering fit of his charcoal-grey pinstripe suit and the impressive way he held himself—with casual grace underlined by strength.

She might have been tired but she wasn't dead, and when he reached the taxi and swivelled to face her, appearing surprised she hadn't kept up, she quickly raised her gaze from where it had been hovering around his body and forced a smile, hoping he couldn't see the surge of uncharacteristic heat in her cheeks.

Bria glanced at her watch, roughly estimating that they were ten minutes away from the hotel, and she was rather grateful.

Since the initial small talk with Sam they'd lapsed into silence, and while it wasn't uncomfortable it was a tad disconcerting to be confined this closely with a guy like him.

A guy like what? Intelligent, articulate and suave?

She may be going through a dating drought

by choice, but she wasn't completely oblivious to a sexy guy, and she could think of worse ways to while away the time between the airport and her destination.

'How long are you staying at the hotel?'

'Just a few days. The conference ends on Sunday after my presentation, but I'm staying on for an extra day. I heard they have a fabulous day spa there, so I thought a little R and R would be a good idea. And you?'

Not that she particularly cared. Sam was one of those guys that flitted in and out of places, focussed on business and little else. She could tell. If he were any other type of guy he would've been talking non-stop to impress her—usually about himself—or pushing her for a date. Instead, he'd done her the courtesy of staying silent for most of the trip.

'I'm staying tonight and tomorrow.'

Surprised and somewhat concerned by the tiny flicker of disappointment at his words, she said, 'That's what I call a flying visit.'

He shrugged, drawing her attention to his broad shoulders beneath a crisp pale-blue tailored shirt.

'Part of the business, I'm afraid. I'm used to it.'

She nodded, understanding completely. Her schedule often included regular flights to all parts of the globe, and she'd fine-tuned a jet-lag cure to cope with it.

In fact, Sam looked damn good for a guy who'd spent over a day on a plane, so he'd obviously discovered his own magical cure for biological-clock warfare, too.

'Do you have any plans tonight?'

She shook her head, envisaging that long soak in the tub she'd been hankering for since the airport.

'In that case, I'd be honoured if you would have dinner with me.'

An instant refusal sprang to her lips. She never dined or flirted, or did much of anything other than focus on work these days, and having dinner with Sam, no matter how nice he'd been, was out of the question.

However, the longer he stared at her with those compelling dark eyes, the more her resolve wavered.

There was nothing sleazy in his invitation, merely a polite request from someone who had already done her a favour by letting her share his taxi.

Why shouldn't she have dinner with him?

She had to eat, hadn't she?

Besides, she sensed a kindred spirit in Sam— someone who was so business-oriented that it was rare to take time out to speak to another human, let alone eat with them.

'I hear that Joseph's restaurant has a world-renowned chef who spent many years in London. Sampling the cuisine would be a must. And I would love to hear more about your presentation. I'm intrigued. It might give me some ideas to improve my own business.'

'In that case, how can I refuse?'

She smiled, surprised at how quickly she'd capitulated, more so by the quick glint of pleasure in Sam's eyes.

He didn't appear smug or sneaky, or any of the things she'd come to look for when guys asked her out. Instead, he seemed genuinely pleased she'd accepted his invitation, and suddenly she looked forward to tonight.

If there was one thing she was comfortable discussing it was her business, and why shouldn't she help Sam out? She owed him for the taxi ride.

Dinner would be like the countless other business meals she'd shared with strangers who'd ended up being her clients.

No pressure. No expectations. Just the way she liked it.

Pleased with the way she'd rationalised her acceptance of Sam's invitation, she sat back and watched as they pulled up outside the beautiful hotel.

'I'll make the reservations. Does eight suit?'

'Fine,' she said, returning his smile, a small part of her recognising she'd never looked forward to dinner with clients as much as she was looking forward to dinner with this enigmatic stranger.

CHAPTER TWO

BRIA entered the restaurant a few minutes early, confident she'd be the first one there. However, the moment she stepped into the elaborate room with velvet banquettes, brushed-silver table lamps and polished mahogany, she saw Sam rise to his feet from a far table and weave his way through the room, his dark eyed gaze fixed solely on her.

She swallowed, unprepared for the rush of excitement, the little thrill of anticipation that this incredible-looking guy was dining with her. Women's heads turned as he strode between the tables, not that she could blame them.

He'd changed out of his business suit into black trousers and an open-necked white shirt which accentuated his deep tan. Though his mannerisms and accent screamed British, she guessed he had a Mediterranean background, what with his dark good looks and unusual surname.

'I'm so glad you joined me,' he said as he reached her side, his appreciative stare sending warmth spiralling through her body. She stiffened, not used to the uncharacteristic physical reaction to a guy, especially one she wouldn't see after tonight.

'Thanks for asking me.'

His eyebrow flicked upward at her short, clipped response, and she inwardly sighed, knowing this was a bad idea.

So she felt slightly indebted to the guy for sharing his taxi with her—that didn't mean she'd had to agree to his dinner invitation. She could've said a polite 'thank you' like the super-cautious woman she usually was and left it at that.

Instead, she'd dithered over her wardrobe choice for five minutes too long—exactly four minutes longer than she usually took—and had that weird, quivering sensation in her belly that dinner with an attractive man for the first time in ages might bring her more than she bargained for.

'You seem a little tense. Are you tired?'

She shook her head, impressed by his perceptiveness, surprised by his consideration. Most guys wouldn't have noticed she was tired.

'Actually, I'm starving. The tiredness is par for the course with my business at the moment.'

He inclined his head, a strangely formal gesture that added to his appeal rather than diminishing it.

'I understand. Please, let us eat so you can retire early.'

Stifling a smile at his formal way of

speaking, she fell into step beside him, acutely aware of his hand resting in the small of her back, gently guiding her through the maze of tables.

Heat seeped through the silk of her dress and her skin prickled, utterly aware of his barely-there touch and reacting accordingly.

Thankfully, they reached their table in record time, and Bria slid into the seat he held out for her, wondering if this was all a smooth, elaborate act or if Sam was this polite all the time.

Not that it mattered. She'd never fallen for a slick charmer before—her ex Ellis had been reserved and a tad bumbling, which is why she'd let him into her life—and she had no intention of loosening up now, even if he did have the most amazing, soulful dark eyes.

She had to admit his eyes fascinated her: the darkest of chocolate brown, mysterious, mesmerising.

Eyes that held secrets.

Eyes possessing wisdom beyond their years.

Eyes hinting at a whole host of possibilities she couldn't begin to fathom.

'Is there something wrong?'

She jolted upright and hoped she hadn't been drooling.

'I'm sorry for staring. That was rude of me.'

And stupid—very, very stupid.

He smiled, and the slight upward turning of his lips softened his face, creating a tiny road-map of lines around those fascinating eyes.

'On the contrary, I'll take it as a compliment. To have a beautiful woman stare at a man is the highest form of flattery.'

'Or insanity.'

The words popped out before she could stop them, but thankfully he laughed.

'You are a very frank woman. I find that intriguing.'

'It becomes irritating after a while. Or so I've been told.'

She picked up a menu and ducked behind it, feeling awkward and gauche and out of her depth with a guy of Sam's class. Rather ironic, considering she'd attended the best of Swiss boarding schools and had mingled with politicians, moguls and the upper echelons of society her entire life.

Yet there was something about him, more than his fancy clothes, posh accent and formal speech patterns, some sort of inbred class that stood him head and shoulders above everyone else.

And that alone should have her running as far from the magnetic property-developer as she could get. Class and power were often inexorably linked, often used to control and manipulate and impress.

She should know.

'Please do not be embarrassed. I value honesty, especially as we have so little time together. Let us share a meal, enjoy each other's company and talk some more.'

The elaborate print of the menu faded before

her eyes as the implication of his smooth words sunk in. The eating part she could do, the enjoyment part was up for debate. As for talking some more, what was so interesting about small talk with a virtual stranger?

Thankfully, the appearance of a waiter put paid to any further chit chat and she placed her order quickly, hoping the black-lip abalone steak tasted as good as it sounded. She usually adored good food, but had a sneaking suspicion that tonight everything would taste like chaff under Sam's disconcerting gaze.

Once the waiter disappeared Sam leaned back in his chair, the simple action drawing his shirt across his chest, and she struggled not to stare at the sheer breadth of it. It was probably as tanned as the rest of him, if the tantalising V of flesh where the collar lay open at his throat was any indication.

'I'm interested in hearing about your business. Can you tell me more about it?'

Bria smiled, inwardly chalking up another brownie point to Sam. Guys weren't usually interested in hearing about her, especially her business. Some neanderthal had once told her he found women talking about business emasculating; needless to say she hadn't lasted to the main course on that date.

Clasping her hands in her lap to stop from fiddling with the cutlery, she said, 'I started up my architectural firm a while back. Motive is my pride and joy. Before that I attended the University of Sydney, completed my degree in architecture, was lucky enough to serve a year under one of Australia's top designers, then branched out on my own.'

She omitted the part about endless arguments with her dad or the countless hours she'd spent trying to convince him she hadn't needed the backing of Kurt Green, Australia's answer to Bill Gates.

Though, there was a difference. Bill worked

for his money whereas her arrogant, lazy father had never lifted a finger a day in his life, other than to point it at her and accuse her of being a failure once he'd realised she wouldn't submit to his control.

'That's very impressive. You must have quite a reputation to be invited as guest speaker at a conference?'

If he only knew.

Sure she had a reputation, as a ballsy, driven workaholic who could turn a dump into a palace. She'd designed some of the biggest, most eye-catching projects in Australia, and had been catapulted to the top of the architectural heap so fast her head still spun.

However, being at the top came at a price, and the long, lonely hours between midnight and six a.m. weren't so great no matter how many times she lay in bed reliving her business success in her head.

She shrugged, not surprised to find her

fingers tugging at the edges of the tablecloth. She always fiddled when she was nervous or uncomfortable, and in the face of Sam's obvious admiration she was definitely uncomfortable.

'I've been lucky. I've designed some fairly well-known projects, and Motive is growing all the time. Not boasting, or anything, but it's bordering on becoming quite famous in this country because of it.'

'We make our own luck,' he said, staring at her intently as the waiter returned, filled their glasses with pricey champagne and left as unobtrusively as he'd arrived.

Though she couldn't fathom the curiosity in his eyes, she agreed one hundred percent about the luck thing.

She might have been born into the richest family in Australia, but she'd shunned that life when old enough to escape her father's clutches, had made her own way in the world, built her own company, and was still her own woman.

Picking up her flute, she raised it in his direction. 'To luck.'

'To luck,' he said, clinking glasses with her ever so softly, his warm, melted-treacle gaze in stark contrast to the icy bite of champagne bubbles sliding down her suddenly constricted throat.

With an extremely handsome guy staring at her with ill-concealed fascination, she felt extremely lucky indeed.

Bria kicked off her stilettos as soon as she entered her room and, padding across to the king-sized bed, flopped back onto the plump pillows.

She was exhausted.

Not a totally foreign feeling, considering she felt this way most nights after the gruelling hours she kept and the way she pushed herself at work, but tonight was different.

Her weariness had nothing to do with work—it had been the furthest thing from her mind for most of the evening—and had everything to do with the suave man who'd held her captivated for most of it.

Sam was something else.

From the top of his thick, black hair to the soles of his polished designer shoes, he'd held her enthralled. He'd said all the right things, done all the right things, and she'd found herself hanging on his every word towards the end of dinner.

Not that he'd said terribly much. Instead he'd steered the conversation away from himself and had focussed it solely on her. She would've normally found such secrecy troubling, and intense scrutiny unnerving, yet when he'd stared at her with that melt-me gaze she'd quite happily blabbed away until she'd stuffed food into her mouth to shut up.

When Sam had talked he'd had a distinct way of speaking, a polite, almost formal intonation that leant weight to his words, and she'd wished several times during the course of the evening that they could spend more time together. It had been a long while since any guy had captured her attention so thoroughly, and she wanted to know more.

Groaning, she closed her eyes and flung her arm across them.

Well, she'd got her wish.

Before they'd parted at the lifts in the foyer Sam had said what a lovely time he'd had, and he would really like to spend tomorrow with her before conducting his business and flying out of the country.

She should've said no.

She should've mumbled some excuse about preparing her speech for Sunday.

She should've turned frigid like she had when any guy had come near her since Ellis.

Instead, she'd smiled and blushed and nodded and made a complete fool of herself.

What was she thinking?

'You weren't,' she mumbled, wondering if she could plead a headache tomorrow morning, knowing that would be the wimp's way out.

Since when had she ever done wimpy?

Determined to ignore the niggle of misgiving that she'd just made an impulsive decision with her heart rather than her head, she logged on to her emails, eager to bury herself in business and forget her fascination with Sam and their impending date.

Scanning through the usual requests for quotes, her gaze focussed on one bearing the heading 'Welcome to Adhara'. Her best friend Eloise had been whisked away to live in the tiny desert country since her marriage to royalty, and had been begging her to visit ever since.

However, this email wasn't another of Lou's badgering missives. Instead, it had come from Ned Wilson, her biggest client in Australia—

the media mogul who had a thing for Middle Eastern architecture, and who'd been hounding her every step to turn his Sydney-harbour mansion into a replica of something out of *Arabian Nights*.

Her finger slipped off the laptop's mouse as she read the email. Ned wanted his mansion to be authentic, had discovered the only mosaics he'd consider having in his home, and had booked her a trip to Adhara.

Shaking her head in disbelief, she reread the email. It wasn't a request, it was an order, and considering Ned Wilson could make or break careers—and had done so quite publicly in the past—it looked like she had little choice.

She hated any guy thinking he could control her, yet, with the promise of Ned's renovated mansion sending her reputation through the glass ceiling, she'd swallow her pride for once and do what he wanted. Architecture was predominantly male-oriented and she battled for recognition with every job.

Taking a few calming breaths before she fired off a response, Bria checked out the information Ned had attached to the email. Though she hated his high-handedness in organising this trip without asking, she couldn't help but be fascinated by the sweeping desert sands, the white-washed buildings and the quaint market places.

She'd always been fascinated by exotic places and their architecture, and it looked like she was about to get an up-close-and-personal view of Adhara whether she wanted it or not.

Sighing, she fired off a second email, to Lou this time, informing her of the upcoming visit. Her friend would be ecstatic, though considering the business nature of the trip she seriously doubted they'd have much time for doing what they loved best: lounging around, sharing gossip and packets of chocolate Tim-Tams.

All in all, this trip wouldn't be too bad. Ned could've sent her to the outer reaches of the Sahara on a whim, rather than a country where she knew someone, and once she completed his house her reputation as an architect would soar.

Nothing like positive publicity to build a career, she thought, and, feeling more upbeat than she had a few minutes ago, Bria logged off and padded into the bathroom, her mind filled with images of endless stretches of desert—quickly replaced by a man with mesmerising dark eyes.

CHAPTER THREE

'How gorgeous.'

Bria's first glimpse of the Victorian rose garden took her breath away.

At least, that was her excuse and she was sticking to it.

No way could the slight breathless feeling tightening her chest have anything to do with the guy by her side, no matter how perfect he seemed.

'I agree. Gorgeous,' Sam said, his dark-eyed gaze fixed firmly on her, and not wavering towards the beautiful blooms for a second.

Heat crept into her cheeks, and Bria silently chastised herself for reacting like a blushing schoolgirl to a compliment from a suave man.

So, Sam had charm. She'd figured that out pretty quick-smart over dinner last night, and for guys like him paying compliments didn't mean a thing. It came as naturally to them as breathing.

'Shall we keep walking?'

She barely waited for his nod, eager to escape the enigmatic smile playing about his mouth as she headed into the garden. Losing herself among the stunning blooms would be infinitely better than losing herself in the seductive power of his smile.

'There is so much colour, so much beauty,' he said, his reverent tone stopping her in her tracks, and she turned, surprised to see him stooping low and inhaling the fragrance of a magnificent red rose the size of a fist.

She'd never expected an international businessman to take time out to smell the roses, literally, and seeing Sam softly caress the petals of the perfect blood-red bloom brought an unexpected lump to her throat.

Oh, no… No, no, no!

She didn't do emotion when it came to guys, never had, and, considering she'd barely known Sam twenty-four hours, letting him breach the iron-clad barriers around her heart would be beyond foolish.

Men were great in the boardroom, so-so in the bedroom, and had no clues when it came to her needs. Which was why she'd eventually tired of Ellis, no matter how convenient it had been to share some of her life with him in London.

Considering his true colours, she'd been lucky she hadn't let him into her heart despite the occasional yearning for something more, something beyond the rather cool relationship they'd had.

As for Sam, falling for a guy she barely knew

would be the ultimate insanity, especially considering he lived on the opposite side of the planet and was a walking, talking advertisement for everything she mistrusted in a guy.

Clearing her throat, she grabbed at a nice, safe topic to clear her befuddled head.

'I'm off on a really interesting trip once this conference is finished,' she said, unable to stop her gaze drifting to his butt as he bent over the rose, knowing it wasn't the tailored fit of his casual khaki trousers that held it but the perfection outlined beneath the cotton.

'Where are you going?'

He straightened and she shifted her gaze in record time, the heat in her cheeks intensifying as he locked gazes with her, and she had the uncanny feeling he could read her mind.

'You probably haven't heard of it. It's a tiny country called Adhara. One of my clients is mad for Middle Eastern architecture and wants his house to be perfect, so has basically ordered me to go over there. Plus, my best friend lives there, so it should be great.'

Sam stiffened, his gaze snapping to hers before he smiled, a genuinely warm smile which reached his eyes and turned them to molten chocolate, despite the flicker of something mysterious in their depths.

'Actually, I have heard of it. It's a beautiful country.'

'You've been there?'

He hesitated a moment before nodding.

'My business takes me to many places in the world. It's one of the perks.'

'Same here,' she said, wondering if she could pump him for more information than she'd gleaned from the stuff Ned had sent through last night.

Adhara piqued her curiosity, and from what she'd seen of the desert land on the Net she knew designing the perfect house for Ned Wilson would be a challenge she was more than up for.

'Though I must admit travelling to a place like Adhara wouldn't have been my first choice, unless I was practically ordered to go.'

'Why?'

Bria shrugged, somewhat disconcerted by Sam's penetrating stare, more so by her compulsion to divulge her thoughts to a man she barely knew.

'Honestly? From the snippets I've gleaned from Lou, my best friend, I have this vision of a tiny country something along the lines of Monaco. You know, the type of place ruled by an insular, powerful family controlling everyone and everything. I guess I've never gone in for that sort of thing.'

Sam's lips thinned, as if he didn't approve of her thoughts. Not surprising, considering he was an influential businessman living in London who probably thrived on controlling everything, from his work to his social life.

'If you haven't been there how can you judge the country?'

If his grim expression hadn't been a dead giveaway that he didn't approve, the bitter edge to his words would.

'I suppose you think I'm way too judge-mental, huh?'

She deliberately kept her tone light, not wanting anything to spoil the special day they'd had.

It had definitely been far too long since she'd spent any time with a guy, let alone one as im-pressive as Sam, and she'd lost her ability to keep things cool.

'Everyone is entitled to their own views,' he said, the tension in his shoulders relaxing as he stepped to her side. 'But I will be interested to hear what you think of Adhara once you're there.'

'Uh-huh,' she mumbled, knowing that wouldn't happen.

She wouldn't keep in touch with Sam.

What was the point?

London and Sydney were poles apart. She'd already tried living on the other side of the world once before, and look where that had got her.

'Shall we have our picnic now?'

Glad to hear Sam's jovial tone, she nodded and looked up, surprised by the glint of purpose in his eyes.

His gaze was too potent.

He was standing too close.

And when she took a deep breath to clear her head his subtle scent, faintly reminiscent of sandalwood mingled with the heady rose fragrance surrounding them, had her leaning towards him to savour more.

'Bria?'

He reached out and placed a finger beneath her chin, gently tilting her head up till she had no option but to stare into his eyes, mesmerised by the flicker of excitement in their obsidian depths.

A sizzle of heat licked along her veins, making her want to close the short distance between them, plant her lips against his and see if they tasted as good as they looked.

He had a finely shaped mouth, the type of mouth made for delivering important news, for imparting smooth words, for soul-deep, soul-destroying kisses…

'Shall we eat now?'

He spoke so softly she barely heard, and through the fog of insane need clouding her brain she registered several fleeting thoughts at once.

I want to kiss him.

I want to know more about him.

I want to spend more time with him.

Instead, she stepped away, breaking the tenuous contact between them, knowing what she wanted and what she got were usually at opposite ends of her life's spectrum.

'Sounds good. I'm starving,' she said, heading for the picnic blanket they'd set up under a nearby oak tree, more than a little annoyed this man had the power to breach her emotional barriers without trying.

'Your country is beautiful.'

Bria tore her gaze from the magnificent setting sun and turned towards Sam, as dazzled by his gorgeousness as the purple, ochre and golden dusk descending around them.

'It is. They don't call Australia "the lucky country" for nothing.'

An indefinable emotion flickered in the dark depths of his eyes before he smiled.

'At this moment I am the lucky one.'

Bria returned his smile, revelling in the splendour of the moment, knowing it was too late to play coy or pretend she didn't understand what he implied.

She'd spent the most incredible, magical day with Sam, and the sparks sizzling between them had been difficult to ignore. He hadn't overstepped the mark once, and she'd had to physically refrain from launching herself at him several times.

How ironic she was emotionally frigid yet so responsive physically to his potent presence.

'Are you flattering me?'

He shrugged, the simple action pulling his white polo-shirt up, and displaying a tantalising glimpse of flat, tanned stomach for an all-too-brief second.

'I am merely stating the truth.'

'So you've enjoyed today?'

His steady stare sent a ripple of awareness down her spine.

'More than you could possibly know.'

'I've had a good time too,' she said, turning back to lean on the elaborate balustrade of the Mansion, concentrating on the view before she burned up from the inside out.

Not dating for so long had been a stupid move, if this was how she reacted to a guy after knowing him for less than two days. She never behaved like this, she usually made sure of it.

Isolating her heart, protecting her emotions, were learned responses and they'd served her just fine. No use tampering with a foolproof survival mechanism, no matter how tempting the guy.

'It is a shame it has to end.'

She couldn't agree more but, the sooner she put an end to her whimsical, nonsensical yearning where Sam was concerned, the better.

Instilling the right amount of regret into her voice, she said, 'Yes, but I must prepare my presentation tonight.'

'Your work is very important to you. I understand.'

The surprising thing was she could tell he did understand. There was no censure in his tone, no judgement, and she wished for the hundredth time that day that things could be different.

'Would you like to walk back to the hotel now?'

She could add 'intuitive' to his list of already growing, impressive attributes.

Fiddling with a patch of peeling paintwork on the balustrade, she furiously marshalled her thoughts, knowing she should end this now and walk away alone.

She hated goodbyes, hated the awkwardness that accompanied them, and she knew without a doubt that saying goodbye to Sam would be harder than she could've thought possible when they'd first met at the airport yesterday.

'Bria? Is something wrong?'

Sighing, she turned to face him, torn between wanting to make a run for it and prolonging their parting for as long as possible.

'Honestly? I've enjoyed your company more than I expected, and I've always found saying goodbye difficult.'

He raised an eyebrow, the corners of his mouth curving up into a smile.

'I think you just paid me a compliment.'

'You bet,' she muttered under her breath, wishing her pulse wouldn't accelerate at the slightest glimpse of his smile, all too aware she'd never had this instant attraction to any other man before, and totally thrown by it.

'If saying goodbye is so difficult, maybe we should agree to meet again?'

Her heart turned over in hope before plummeting. She may be in the throes of forgetting every sane reason why she usually held guys like Sam at bay, but that didn't mean she'd lost it completely.

Keeping in contact would be futile, considering this was a flying visit to Australia for him and she had no plans to return to London any time soon.

Not to mention the unshakeable fear that her interest in him, and the incredible speed at which it had developed, could breach the finely honed defence mechanisms she'd taken a lifetime to establish.

Shaking her head, she said, 'I don't think that's going to happen, so maybe it's best we say goodbye now?'

Rather than his smile slipping, it widened into a confident grin of a guy used to getting everything he wanted.

'I asked you yesterday if you believed in fate.'

'And I'm pretty sure I told you what I think of it,' Bria said, finding his philosophising strange in a man who obviously dealt in concrete deals on a daily basis.

The businessmen she liaised with were firmly rooted in facts and figures, relegating fate to the hands of those unlucky enough to lose out to their mega deals. Yet here Sam was, implying there was something more to their meeting than a chance encounter—weird.

'Do you want to know what I think?'

Her breath hitched as he took a step closer, filling her personal space with his potent presence, drawing her towards him like metal to a magnet.

'Uh-huh.'

'I think we're going to meet again. Soon.'

She chuckled at his prediction, her forced laughter a cover for the riotous nerves pulsating through her body at his proximity.

She wanted to flee.

She wanted to stay.

She didn't know what the heck she wanted!

Sam took the decision out of her hands when he reached out and captured her face between his palms.

'This has been a special time for me, Bria Green. And I think you feel the same way.'

She couldn't nod, couldn't speak, couldn't think, and when he leaned forward and brushed his lips against hers in the barest of kisses her eyelids fluttered shut as sensation exploded like a fireball.

'That is fate's way of sealing our future

meeting,' he murmured, his deep voice washing over her in a sensuous wave, low, warm, intimate, and she all but melted against him.

His lips grazing hers had sent her lingering doubts of a proper goodbye up in flames and she opened her eyes, determined to imprint this man, this moment, in her mind.

However, the instant her eyes opened her resolution to make their farewell short and sweet vanished and she covered his mouth with hers, pouring her incredible, uncharacteristic desire for him into the swift, heartfelt kiss.

She didn't think.

She didn't rationalise.

She didn't excuse.

Instead, the minute he responded by parting his lips a fraction she deepened the kiss, eager to taste him, to tease him, to drive him wild with wanting.

As much as she wanted this kiss, as much as she wanted him.

Fire streaked through her body as their tongues touched, tentatively at first, before growing more eager, more demanding.

He tasted of the sweet strawberries dipped in chocolate they'd shared for their picnic dessert, an intoxicating combination she'd never forget.

Sam infused her with sensations she'd never dreamed possible. She wanted to taste him, to feel him, to hear him moan her name...

He groaned and slid his fingers into her hair, pushing her hard up against the balustrade as he showed her exactly how much their attraction was mutual.

Bria had no idea how long they stood there, mouths frantic, bodies entwined, but the moment he broke the kiss reality came crashing down with a finality that left her more breathless, if that were possible.

She'd thrown herself at him.

She'd practically devoured him.

What had she been thinking?

Racking her brain for the right words, for any words, she gnawed at her bottom lip.

'You do not need to say anything,' Sam said, placing a finger against her lips for an all-too-brief moment, before dropping his hand.

Cursing her ineptitude with men, she said, 'Sam, I—'

'We will meet again. Trust me.'

Shaking her head, she said, 'You're a very confident guy, but I have to disagree with you on this one.'

He shrugged and she fisted her hands to prevent herself from reaching out and feeling those broad shoulders one last time.

'Then let us agree to disagree. Shall we return to the hotel now?'

Hating that the inevitable moment had finally come, Bria squared her shoulders and looked him straight in the eye in the same way she'd faced any unpleasant situation for as long as she could remember.

'I'd rather head back alone, if that's okay with you?'

He inclined his head in a strangely formal gesture. 'As you wish.'

Taking a steadying breath, and battling an annoying burning at the back of her eyes, she said, 'Take care. I hope you enjoyed your visit to Melbourne.'

His eyes glittered with pleasure, and she took a small step back to stop launching into his arms again.

'I most certainly did. Thank you for spending time with me.'

'It was fun.'

Fun? *Fun?* Could she be any more under-stated if she tried?

'Farewell, Bria Green.'

He took her hand and bent over it, placing a soft, lingering kiss on the back of it, and she sighed, wishing she could prolong this moment for ever.

'Bye, Sam.'

Smiling into his handsome face for the last time, she couldn't fathom his triumphant expression or the mysterious gleam in his chocolate eyes and, forcing her legs to move, she walked away.

Her kitten heels tapping against the polished veranda-boards echoed in the eerie silence, and she willed herself not to look back despite the overwhelming urge to do just that.

'This is not goodbye,' Sam said, his tone sure and commanding, and her steps faltered as a shiver ran up her spine.

She might not believe in fate or premonition, or any of that stuff, but in that second, with the taste of Sam lingering on her lips and the precious memories of their brief time together in her heart, she almost wished she did.

CHAPTER FOUR

'BREE, over here.'

Bria's head swivelled to the tall, elegant brunette stepping out of a gleaming silver limousine, excitement making her forget her luggage as she flew across the scorching concrete.

'Lou! You look amazing!'

Lou laughed and cried and squeezed the life out of her as they hugged, and stepped apart for a second before hugging again.

'It's so good to see you, Bree.'

Lou held her at arm's length, her mischievous blue stare travelling over Bria's mint-green shift dress and matching shoes in record time.

'And wearing Prada, no less.'

Bria laughed and slapped her hands away. 'You haven't changed a bit. Still the label queen, huh?'

Lou pouted and stuck out a hip.

'Does this look designer to you?'

'Actually, no, but it looks divine all the same.'

'It's a *salwaar kameez*. They're super-comfortable.'

Bria had never seen her friend wearing Middle Eastern clothing, and the long, loose trousers with matching tunic in ice blue brocaded with silver accentuated her elegance.

'I can't believe you're actually here.'

Lou's eyes welled for a moment, and a shaft of guilt pierced Bria's happiness.

The two of them had been through a lot, from surviving the strict rules at the stuffy Swiss boarding school her dad had insisted she attend to tearing up London on a year-long fun fest.

Lou had been there for her through the Ellis

break-up, she knew how bad things were with her dad, yet Bria had held off visiting her best friend because of her constant quest to be the best in her career.

Pretty selfish.

'About time, huh?'

'Way past time.' Lou rolled her eyes and enveloped her in another bear-hug. 'Now that you're here, what do you want to do? We can spend the night at Burl Al Arab, the most amazing hotel in the world right here in Dubai, or we can head straight to Adhara. Your call.'

'I'd rather make tracks to Adhara. After all the research material I've seen, I'm curious.'

'Great.' Lou clapped her hands in a classic excited gesture Bria remembered from all their school exploits—and there'd been many. 'Bet you're glad I'm still living at the royal residence.'

'Too right. I'd much rather stay there than the hotel Ned organised. It's not every day a girl gets to live in a palace.'

Images of tall, white spires, soft rounded domes and curved mosaic-framed windows set against the backdrop of endless desert sprang to mind. Despite her initial anger at being forced to visit Adhara by a pushy client, she had to admit that seeing the palace pictures Lou had emailed her after she'd told her of her visit had whetted her architectural appetite.

'Will the prince mind me staying?'

Lou shrugged. 'I have no idea. We barely see him. Yusif handles some of his business interests here in the Middle East, but the Prince spends most of his time abroad. He's a real go-getter.'

'What's he like?'

Not that Bria was particularly interested, but if she happened to run into royalty while she was here she'd like to be well prepared, and not make any *faux pas* or cause any international incidents.

To her surprise, a blush accompanied her friend's smirk.

'You've heard of princes and their playboy reputations? Well, His Royal Highness is something else.'

'In what way?'

Lou's grin widened. 'If you're lucky enough you'll find out.'

Bria knew that smile. It was the same goofy smile her friend had worn for years whenever a hot guy had hovered around.

'So he's not old, decrepit and wrinkly?'

'Far from it!'

They laughed and leaned into one another like they had a million times before, and once again Bria was struck by how much she'd missed this, how much she'd missed Lou.

'Come on. Let's hit the road. We'll need to change from the limo to four-wheel drive on the outskirts of Dubai, and it'll take us another six hours to get to Adhara.'

'Lead the way.'

Bria froze momentarily as she slid into the

limo's cool leather interior, assailed by recent memories of how refusing to do just this had resulted in a memorable meeting with a man she couldn't forget, no matter how hard she tried.

'What's up?'

Lou turned an ever-astute gaze on her, and Bria briefly wondered if Sam was worth mentioning.

'Come on, Bree, we've got hours to kill, so you may as well spill the goss.'

Sighing, Bria leaned back against the comfy leather headrest.

What could she say—she was interested in a guy she'd barely known for two days? A guy she'd probably never see again, despite his prophesising to the contrary.

Lou squealed. 'You've met someone, haven't you? Come on, I want to hear every last, juicy detail.'

Smiling, Bria said, 'There's not much to tell, actually. We met briefly at the conference I told you about. Had dinner the first night, spent a pretty romantic day together the next, and that was it.'

Apart from that one scintillating farewell kiss she couldn't forget…

'What do you mean, that was it? Aren't you going to see him again?'

Bria shook her head, wishing she didn't feel so lousy at the thought of not basking in the heat of Sam's chocolate gaze ever again.

'He lives in London. I live in Sydney. End of story.'

Lou rolled her eyes. 'What is it with you and London guys?'

'You promised me you'd never refer to *him* again, remember?'

The mere thought of Ellis and the time she'd wasted trying to make a go of their relationship had her ready to run screaming into the desert.

'Good point.'

Lou paused for a second but Bria could tell

it wouldn't be for long, not with her friend's blue eyes gleaming.

'But as for this new guy… I haven't heard you mention a guy in the last two years, let alone go on a date with anyone, so he has to be something. As for the distance thing, ever heard of email, phone calls, even flying to visit?'

Bria waved away the suggestions, hating the fact she'd contemplated them all herself many times on the long flight from Australia to Dubai.

'Too complicated. Besides, long-distance relationships aren't my thing.'

'Relationships aren't your thing full-stop, since that dweeb Ellis. Not every guy's like him, and it's about time you gave yourself a break.'

'It wasn't all his fault, you know. I basically went into that relationship to test the waters, to see if anything could develop between us.'

Lou snorted. 'The guy was a cold fish and

had dollar signs in his eyes. You wanted to make a go of it, he wanted the prestige the Green name could bring him. He was a creep.'

'Yeah, he was, wasn't he?'

Bria laughed, though she knew deep down that her failed, brief relationship with Ellis hadn't entirely been his fault.

She rarely dated, preferring to concentrate on building her business, and, considering she had no intention of ever marrying, she'd let Ellis move in with her almost on a whim, like some strange type of sociological experiment.

He'd been polite, cultured and deferential—the clincher as far as she'd been concerned. A go-get-'em guy would've tried to control her, just like her dad had always done, and there was no way she'd go near a guy like that.

Then what are you doing remembering Sam?

Determinedly ignoring that question, she turned towards Lou who was snapping her fingers under her nose.

'So, what about this mystery man? Think you'll follow him up?'

'We'll see,' Bria said, eager to end this conversation. For the longer Lou egged her on about Sam the more her resolve would waver, and she might do something crazy like ring the number Sam had scribbled on a nondescript card and had left for her at Reception before his departure.

Thankfully, the limo drew to a smooth halt at that moment, and Lou bundled her out of the limo and into the equally impressive four-wheel-drive vehicle waiting for them.

Good. A long drive in the desert would give her plenty of time to grill Lou about her life in Adhara, and ample opportunity to keep her mind off guys with model-handsome faces and piercing dark eyes.

Bria's breath caught at her first glimpse of the royal residence.

Nothing could've prepared her for the splendour of the white-washed domes and spires silhouetted against the golden desert sands stretching to the horizon, where the sun, a fiery purple-and-magenta ball, dipped and slid slowly from view.

Neither the pictures Ned and Lou had forwarded her nor her friend's glowing recommendations had prepared her for the breathtaking beauty before her, and she sighed, spellbound.

'Pretty impressive, huh?'

Bria heard the pride in Lou's voice, and couldn't blame her. If she lived in a place like this she'd be bursting with pride too.

' "Wow" doesn't begin to come close, does it?'

Lou laughed. 'Now you know why I've been trying to drag you over here for the last year. The place is magical.'

It would have to be, to have turned her fun-loving, jet-setting best friend into the kind of subservient wife a prince's cousin would probably demand, the type of woman Bria's mother had become since marrying her father—the type of woman Bria had vowed never to be.

'So does it appeal to your architectural eye?'

Bria smiled. 'What do you think?'

The closer they got, the more she couldn't tear her eyes away from the ornate dome-shaped windows framed in exquisite turquoise-and-ruby mosaic, the terracotta doors in ancient wood, and the curved whitewashed stone walls.

This place was an architect's dream, and she could easily spend a year here studying every exquisite line and curve.

'It's huge,' Bria said as the four-wheel drive drove around the back, through an elaborate, carved wooden gate manned by armed guards, and pulled up outside a matching door.

'Wait till you see the rest. You'll be doubly glad you ditched that client's hotel in exchange for a stay in a palace.'

Lou grinned and almost leaped from the car, her excitement infectious as Bria nodded and followed, eager to take a look inside. If the outside was anything to go by, she was in for a real treat.

Heading to the back of the car, she waited for the driver to unlock the rear door so she could grab her bags and start exploring. However, the driver didn't share her impatience. Instead, he stood in front of her, arms folded, a frown creasing his brow as his confused gaze flicked from her to Lou.

'Come on, Bree. Leave the bags. They'll be taken straight up to your room.'

Bria stiffened, recalling unpleasant memories of similar conversations with her dad, where she'd do anything to subvert his control.

'It's fine, I can take my own bags up.'

Lou strolled back to the car, her casual, elegant strides in stark contrast to the feverish pace her friend used to maintain. She draped an arm around Bria's shoulders and bent to whisper in her ear.

'Look, I know you loathe all these trappings of wealth, but while you're here you'll have to go with the flow, okay? It's a way of life at the palace, and you don't want to confuse the Adharans who work here or, worse, insult them?'

Bria didn't budge. However, the last thing she wanted to do was get any of the locals offside considering Lou lived among them. Lou's friendship was priceless and she wouldn't jeopardise it, despite her bitter memories of a time she'd rather forget.

'Fine,' Bria said, rewarded by one of Lou's brilliant smiles and a stiff nod from the driver as she turned away from the car and followed Lou into the palace.

It wasn't often she got to combine business with pleasure, and she had every intention of doing both this trip.

* * *

Bria blinked, closed her eyes and reopened them, turning a slow three-sixty in the centre of the room.

She may have grown up privileged and surrounded by the finer things in life, but nothing came close to the sheer opulence of this room.

Her *bedroom*?

Chuckling, she shook her head at the understatement. The room, boasting a low ochre-and-chocolate sofa set, marble coffee-tables and an exquisite hand-woven rug large enough to cover an entire floor at Harrods, was separated from the king-sized bed, hand-carved wardrobes and massive marble *en suite* by an inlaid Egyptian-like screen which could've divided a mountain range.

The room was beautiful, from the swirling ebony and ruby of the rug, to the matching silk cushions, from the intricate mosaics lining the windows, to the richness of the emerald bedspread. The thought of escaping to this private oasis at any time while she 'worked' over the next few weeks was tempting.

Sinking into the nearest chair and sighing at the cocooning comfort, she closed her eyes, savouring the fragrant scent pervading the room.

She couldn't quite place it: sandalwood? Honey? Orange blossom? Whatever it was, it added to the ambiance and the captivating exoticism.

However, thinking along exotic lines conjured up another vivid image—that of a man with a Mediterranean tan and eyes like coal, a man who'd captured her interest way too quickly, a man she couldn't stop thinking about, despite every effort to the contrary.

'Snap out of it,' she muttered, her eyes flying open at the slight knock at the door.

'Come in,' she said, expecting Lou to drop by and inform her of their plans for the next few days, and surprised by the appearance of a young girl who wouldn't quite meet her eyes.

'Is everything to your liking, Miss Green?'

Bria stood and advanced towards the door, beckoning the girl in.

'Yes, thanks. I'm afraid I haven't met many people yet, so I don't know you. Are you a relative of the Prince?'

The girl blushed, darting a frightened glance over her shoulder.

'No, miss. I am Rasha. I am here to serve you.'

Bria's blood chilled at the murmured words. She'd hated having staff wait on her when growing up, particularly as her dad had used them as another form of control to spy and report back to him, and nothing had changed.

'Serve me?'

Rasha nodded. 'I am your personal maid.'

'But I don't need…' She trailed off, the girl's stricken expression a timely reminder of her earlier discussion with Lou.

She didn't want to offend Rasha, let alone the Prince, and, gritting her teeth, she said, 'I don't need anything right now, thank you.'

Rasha's sudden smile lit up her face. 'But if you do, you know who to call.'

She nodded, silently vowing to keep her use of the eager young woman to a minimum.

'Madame Eloise asked me to give you a message.'

'Yes?'

'She will come to your room in one hour and take you on a tour of this wing.'

Rasha's English was flawless and only slightly accented, and Bria wondered about the education in a country like Adhara. Were girls treated as equally as boys? Did they have the same opportunities?

Unable to stifle her curiosity, Bria said, 'Your English is perfect. Did you learn it at school?'

The young woman blushed and nodded shyly.

'Yes. It is part of our heritage, along with French and Arabic. English is taught in all Adharan schools. Though, I've had a chance to practice more since I've worked for the Prince.'

'He encourages you to speak English?'

Bria's eyebrows shot upwards, and she chuckled as Rasha imitated her surprised expression.

'But of course. The Prince has the country's best interests at heart. He wants us all to be proficient in more than one language, for change is coming.'

'Change?'

Rasha nodded vigorously, her dark eyes glowing with enthusiasm.

'Growth. A larger city. More job opportunities. The Prince is determined to make it all happen. He only wants the best for our country.'

'I see,' Bria said, somewhat intrigued by such a forward-thinking ruler in a country surrounded by old kingdoms ruled by antiquated sheikhs.

'The Prince is a man of honour. You will soon see for yourself.'

'Oh?'

A tiny ripple of unease slid down Bria's spine. She had no intention of speaking to the prince unless she had to, and when Lou had told her earlier that he was rarely around she'd been relieved.

Call her crazy, call her old-fashioned, but she had an image of an arrogant, powerful tyrant with a harem of women trailing after him fixed in her head, and she had no intention of bowing down to any man no matter how welcoming her lodgings.

'His Highness returned this morning. He will probably summon you tomorrow after you are well rested.'

Rasha's matter-of-fact pronouncement didn't rankle half as much as the thought of being 'summoned' by anyone, especially some high-and-mighty ruler.

'But I talk too much. I must leave you to rest. Please do not hesitate to ring for me if you need anything.'

'Thanks,' Bria said, smiling as the girl inclined her head and backed out of the door before closing it as quietly as she'd entered.

She'd enjoyed the illuminating chat with Rasha.

So the Prince of Adhara was progressive and forward thinking?

This she had to see.

CHAPTER FIVE

BRIA TOOK a deep breath, smoothed the front of her cream shot-silk dress and knocked on the door to the Prince's private rooms, wishing she weren't so nervous, when a muffled 'Come in,' had her twisting the elaborate gold knob to enter.

So what if this guy was a prince?

She'd met rulers before—had dined with them, had played with their children. This would be a cinch.

However, as she closed the door behind her and advanced into the room, an uneasy feeling skittered down her spine as she observed the tall man wearing a white dress-uniform and hat, draining a glass before he turned towards her.

There was something familiar about the breadth of his shoulders, the way he replaced the glass on the tray… And as she caught her first glimpse of his profile, her heart stuttered to a stop as she reeled back, landing with a hard thump against the door.

'Bria, I know this must come as a shock. Are you all right?'

She braced against the door, willing her legs to hold her up, willing her heart to restart before she blacked out as spots danced before her eyes, willing her mind to comprehend that the man dressed in a fancy uniform—the man who'd crossed the room in record speed to take hold of her hands and support her, the man now staring at her with growing concern—was Sam.

Sam, the guy who'd intrigued her in Melbourne.

Sam, the guy who'd promised they'd meet again.

Sam, the *Prince?*

The Prince!

Her heart kicked and bucked in her chest like a wild stallion as blood pounded in her veins.

This couldn't be real.

Maybe she had a case of delayed jet-lag.

Maybe she'd been working too hard and was having a mini-breakdown.

'Come and sit down. Let me pour you some tea.'

Blinking like she'd awoken from a coma, Bria allowed the Prince—she couldn't equate him with her Sam just yet—to lead her to a low russet sofa, gently push her down and leave her to pour a glass of mint tea, a drink she'd come to like during her first day here.

'Here. Drink this.'

She took the proffered glass and sipped mechanically, her gaze drawn to his face.

Those hard planes, high cheekbones, dark eyes and sensual lips… She choked, spluttering and coughing as reality hit.

This *was* Sam.

Her Sam.

Sam, the Prince of Adhara, who'd charmed her without trying, who'd lied to her from the very beginning.

And she'd been stupid enough to let down her impenetrable defences to let him into her life, however transiently.

'We need to talk.'

He took the glass from her hand, obviously sensing a shift in her mood as she moved from stunned disbelief to fierce outrage.

Determined to keep her voice steady, she said, 'We need to talk? Hmm, let me see, what shall we talk about? The fact you're not who you said you were? The fact you're a prince? The fact you're playing some weird game, and I seem to be the only player unaware of the rules?'

'I never lied to you.'

'You're kidding, right?'

Bria leaped off the couch like she'd just sat on a scorpion, torn between wanting to run out of the room and wanting to run into his arms as the attraction she'd fought so hard to forget reignited in a second at the sound of his low, familiar voice.

'I never lied to you. I am a property developer. I was in Melbourne on business, gaining ideas for Adhara City. I do live in London for part of the year.'

She swivelled to face him, hating his calm explanation, his cool, well-modulated English tone that had duped her into believing he was something he wasn't.

'And what about the rest?'

The part where he'd charmed her, had flattered her, had kissed her and made her believe for one, tiny, infinitesimal moment that she could learn to trust again.

'The rest?'

'The part about you being a prince and all?'

She finished lamely, refusing to acknowledge she'd opened her heart to him even the tiniest amount.

He shrugged, as if being royalty meant nothing. 'It was not relevant.'

'Not relevant?'

Her voice rose to a high-pitched shriek and she calmed it with effort. 'Is your name even Sam Wali?'

'My full name is Prince Samman al Wali, but most of my friends and family call me Sam.'

Just like that, her anger deflated. Facing Sam in his royal uniform, hearing his real name, hearing him speak in that plummy tone all served to ram home the fact that he was a prince and that the divide between them was irreversible.

Despite all her protests to the contrary, a small part of her had believed Sam in

Melbourne when he'd said they'd meet again. A larger part of her had wished it would happen, and his card had burned a hole in her purse ever since.

How ironic, that after all her dithering over whether to call him or not the decision had been taken out of her hands. And how!

'I know this must come as a shock to you,' he said, stepping around the low-set marble-topped coffee table as if to reach for her, and she held up her hands to ward him off.

'Just tell me this. Did you know Eloise was my best friend back in Melbourne? Did you know who I was at the airport when we first met? Did you have a hand in getting Ned to send me here?'

Her voice shook as the possible extent of his treachery hit, and she sank into the nearest chair, hating to show weakness in front of him, yet unable to stand any longer as weariness seeped through her body.

She'd felt this wobbly, this betrayed, once before—when she'd discovered her father had paid her first boyfriend to escort her to her debutante ball—and she'd vowed back then never to feel so vulnerable again.

Yet here she was, experiencing the same confusion, the same pain.

She just didn't get this, any of it.

Sam sat opposite her, resting an arm across the back of the sofa, his long legs outstretched and ankles crossed. He looked unflappable, supremely confident and totally in charge.

She wanted to hit him.

'I did not know who you were when we first met. I saw an opportunity and I seized it. I do not know this Ned person, but have since learned he is a client of yours through Eloise. And I did not know you had any links to Adhara till much later.'

'But why didn't you say anything, particularly after I told you I would be visiting here?'

He shrugged, a sombre expression on his face.

'I wanted you to come to my country without any ill feelings between us. If I had told you the truth then, you may not have come.'

He'd got that right!

If she'd known she'd be seeing him again, let alone staying at his royal residence, she would never have come.

Liar, her body whispered, as a sudden memory flash of their parting kiss crossed her mind, leaving her slightly breathless.

'You are remembering,' he said, his voice low and husky, in total contrast to the cool, businesslike tone he'd used until that moment.

Her gaze snapped up to his as she fought a rising blush and lost as heat warmed her cheeks.

Damn his eyes: dark, enigmatic, alluring, making her remember when she wanted to forget…

'I don't know what you're talking about,' she murmured, unable to look away no matter how hard she tried, trapped in the mystery of his stare.

'Are you not happy to see me?'

He stood up and stepped around the coffee table with the grace and speed of a gazelle, bending on one knee before her, capturing her hand before she could move, let alone think.

'Even though I omitted to reveal my true identity to you in Melbourne, now that you know, can't you see I am the same man?'

Bria closed her eyes for a moment and shook her head, wishing he'd stop staring at her like she meant something to him, wishing the heat from his gentle touch didn't shoot up her arm and through her body like an electric shock.

'You're not the same.'

His free hand captured her chin and she swallowed, hating the treacherous leap of her heart at their proximity, at being touched by him, no matter how innocuously.

'Look at me,' he said, a simple command she would've disobeyed from sheer habit if it hadn't been for the gentle persuasion in his voice.

Slowly opening her eyes, she stared into his, her pulse pounding in rhythm with her heart, drowning out her voice of sense which repeated every sane reason why she shouldn't be trapped here under the intensity of his stare, his touch burning her skin.

'I am the same. I am the same man who enjoyed your company over dinner. I am the same man who spent a memorable day with you. I am the same man who did this.'

He leaned forward, broaching the small gap between them, and her breath caught as he brushed his lips across hers in a soft, feather-light kiss which had need flowing through her body like liquid lava in an instant.

She should've pushed him away, wrenched free, done something proactive.

Instead she sat there, helpless and wanting, as he slanted his lips across hers again, more demanding this time, coaxing her to respond, and in the split second she had to stop this insanity she threw caution to the wind and kissed him back.

Not softly.

Not gently.

But with all the anger, the passion and slow-burning desire he elicited within her by simply looking at her.

His arms slid around her as her hands made a frantic grab at his hair, coming up with a handful of stiff cotton, and the feel of his hat beneath her fingers acted as an instant dampener.

What was she doing, kissing the Prince of Adhara?

If there had been a minimal chance for her and Sam before, there was absolutely none now. Rulers of countries didn't get involved with average women, and average women didn't fall for rulers who could have any woman in the world.

'You're not the same,' she murmured as she pulled away, sadness creeping into her soul. 'You're not the man I thought you were.'

Sam looked as if she'd struck him before his expression hardened and he recaptured her hands, squeezing tightly.

'I am the same man you met. The same man who is business-focussed like you. The same man who is going to marry you.'

Confusion clouded her brain as Bria tried to process Sam's last comment and failed.

Marry him?

This had to be some kind of joke. The sooner she escaped the palace and the delusional Prince, the better, even if she had to crawl over scorching desert sands to do it.

CHAPTER SIX

As SAM straightened and stepped away Bria stood, needing to face him on equal footing while she confronted him.

He'd had the upper hand till now, pulling the surprise of the century on her with his true identity—closely followed by the shock of his proposal.

Time to turn the tables on His Majesty...or Royal Highness...or whatever a desert prince was called.

'So you're a prince? I can deal with that, but a marriage proposal to a woman you barely know? Are you out of your mind?'

Rather than reacting to her outburst as she expected, he shook his head, a tight smile playing about his mouth, the same mouth that had driven all rational thought from her mind a few moments ago.

'I am perfectly sane,' he said, indicating she should resume her seat with an authoritative sweep of his hand. 'As you will see once we are married.'

In response, she walked behind the chair and folded her arms to prevent herself from doing anything stupid, like shaking some sense into him and creating a national incident.

'Marry you? I don't even know you.'

Sadness mingled with her confusion as she stared him down, determined not to show him how disappointed she was.

For those two wonderful days in Melbourne, she'd thought she had known him, and discovering it had all been an illusion hurt more than it should.

Little wonder she always kept her guard up. Look where it led when she let it slip.

'You know the essentials. I am a man of honour, a man of principle. I will respect you and treat you like a woman deserves to be treated—'

'And how's that—like part of some bevy you probably have stashed away somewhere?'

Humiliation surged through her, swift and bitter, as she realised how close she'd come to being part of that bevy.

'I do not have a bevy. You mustn't listen to rumours about my reputation.'

She stifled a groan as Lou's gossip about him being a playboy flashed into her head.

Great. Not only had she let her guard down for a prince, the guy was a playboy to boot. She knew there was a reason she didn't do emotions—they clouded her judgement, made her feel things she shouldn't, for people she should be wary of.

'I don't care about your reputation. As for you being a prince…'

'Adhara is a progressive country, and I am a modern prince. As such, I need to make the best decisions for my country, and marrying you falls into that category.'

'This is insane.'

Bria whirled and headed for the door, hating the authoritative way he interrupted her, scared beyond belief that for one, infinitesimal second her heart had somersaulted at the idea of being married to a man like Sam.

'This marriage will be beneficial to us both.'

His quiet words uttered with such conviction halted her in her tracks, and she clenched her hands into fists as she swivelled to face him.

'There is nothing you can do or say to convince me that marriage to you would be *beneficial*,' she said, hoping she couldn't be deported for being sarcastic and disrespectful to a prince.

Sam shrugged and held his palms out to her, as if offering her the world.

'You are a career woman, focussed on business, as I am. I can give you worldwide recognition for your work. I can make you the most famous architect in the world.'

Despite her bewilderment, he'd piqued her curiosity with his mention of business.

'And how are you going to do that?'

He smiled, a supremely confident smile of a man used to getting everything he wished for and more.

'Simple. By getting you to design our capital, the new Adhara City. You will be responsible for transforming the city into a show piece—the type of city to rival Dubai, the type of city to draw in tourism and investors and take this country to places it has never been before.'

'You're crazy,' she muttered, shaking her head, hating the flicker of excitement deep in her gut at the thought of a project that big, that challenging.

'No, I can assure you, I am perfectly sane. If you accept my proposal you will be able to pick and choose your work in the future in any country around the world. You will be world-renowned. Able to work for who you want, when you want. Doesn't that tempt you at all?'

Not enough to marry you was her first response, though thankfully she bit her tongue before saying it.

Instead, she fixed him with a haughty stare that hid the bundle of nerves making her belly churn as confusion warred with disbelief.

'None of this makes sense. You're a prince. You're worldly, sophisticated, and way too charming for your own good. You could have any woman you want, a woman of your own social standing, a princess. Why me?'

She needed to know, if for no other reason than to give her beleaguered self-esteem some comfort. If what he'd said was true, he saw her as a business proposition and nothing more, which meant their time together in Melbourne had meant nothing to him.

He smiled, a purely male smile of satisfaction, and her heart thudded in response.

'Because you are perfect for my needs.'

His *needs*?

Bria gulped, hating the instant erotic image that sprung to mind of exactly how she could satisfy his needs.

'And what would a prince who could demand anything possibly need from a woman like me?'

His eyes glittered with untold truths for a moment, before a mask of impassivity slid into place.

'From the first moment I saw you, I knew you were exactly the type of woman I wanted.'

Bria's pulse leapt at the clear intent in his eyes—the same look he'd sent her before kissing her in Melbourne, the same look that could melt her resistance if she lost her mind.

'Don't tell me you orchestrated our meeting at the airport?'

Air rushed from her lungs at the thought she could've been played so completely by this man.

He didn't flinch at her harsh tone. Instead, he sat down and steepled his fingers, resting them against his chest like the self-assured, arrogant male he was.

And she'd been foolish enough to let him into her life.

'I saw a chance when you didn't want to get into that limo, I took it. I overheard your conversation with the chauffeur, when I discovered you were staying at the Mansion, and had my personal assistant arrange it so I would be staying there also. I dismissed my own limousine, secured the last taxi, and you know the rest.'

Her heart sank at the extent of his machinations. Just like her father, he'd manipulated circumstances to control the situation, and in doing so had made her fall in with his plans.

Damn him.

'You still haven't answered my question. Why me? What makes me *exactly the type of woman* you want?'

He ignored her flinging his words back at him, his piercing gaze never leaving her face for an instant as he stood and advanced towards her, the epitome of a supremely confident male in charge of circumstances, of a man who had all the answers.

'You're a woman who doesn't have illusions. Misconceptions will not cloud our union. Our marriage will be based on mutual advancement in our respective business worlds.'

'Wow, when you put it like that, how can a girl refuse?'

She spat out the words, hating that he could present what should be the most romantic moment in the world for a woman in such a cold, callous way.

As for misconceptions clouding anything between them, it was too late for that.

She'd already let him creep under her guard in Melbourne, and her head had spun ever since.

'You do not need to be sarcastic, *gummur*. I am merely stating my proposal in clear terms so there can be no confusion. I'd hoped you would appreciate my honesty and consider my offer.'

Bria wouldn't have been at all surprised if he'd executed a formal little bow to accompany his formal little speech.

As for whatever he'd just called her, it sounded way too intimate coming from his lips, and she wouldn't ask him what it meant no matter how much curiosity burned.

He had it all figured out.

Give her business worldwide notoriety and she'd give him what—a new city?

There had to be more to it.

'Not that I'm considering your offer, but let

me get this straight. This would be a marriage in name only?'

His steady stare did strange things to her pulse, despite the anger still eating away at her.

'I do not think that is what either of us wants.'

Warmth stole through her body at exactly what she wanted from this incredibly sexy man, but she quickly dismissed the thought.

Despite his presumptuous kiss earlier, he'd made it perfectly clear what he wanted: her business acumen.

As for more… Well, it wasn't pertinent, considering she'd never agree to his outlandish proposal.

'Seems to me what I want is pretty irrelevant in this little matrimonial scenario you've conjured up out of thin air. But what about what *you* really want—what your country wants? Won't they expect heirs?'

He paused, studying her face as if trying to

read priceless old scrolls. She waited for him to answer, unaware she was holding her breath till her lungs gave a twinge of protest, and she inhaled deeply, wishing he didn't affect her this way.

She'd been immune to men for so long, had built up a protective shield around her heart, so what was so special about this guy?

Watching his eyes darken with intrigue as his gaze travelled over her with the slow precision of a caress, she had her answer.

'I have already told you. I am modern in my outlook. I want what is best for my country, but I answer to no one. People may expect heirs, I do not. In fact, I have no expectations of this marriage, other than for you to play the role of my wife…in every way.' His eyes glittered with untold promise, and she inadvertently swallowed. 'And design our new city. That is all.'

That wasn't all, and she knew it the second

his gaze left her to fix at some point over her left shoulder.

There *was* more to it, and if there was one thing she liked more than architecture it was a good mystery.

'I will give you one week to ponder your decision.'

Bria opened her mouth to tell Sam where he could stick his proposal once and for all, when he held up his hand swiftly.

'One week. All I ask is you keep an open mind. See what my country has to offer. Tour the city. Immerse yourself in Adharan culture. Spend some time with me—some quality time.'

His voice dropped lower, his smooth-as-caramel tone as mesmerising as the liquid heat of his eyes.

'I will see to it you have no option but to say yes.'

Blinking rapidly to dispel the hypnotic spell

he'd cast over her with his lulling voice, she squared her shoulders, determined to ignore the tiny thrill of anticipation deep inside that being Sam's wife—in every sense of the word—would be beyond pleasurable.

'My answer will always be no.'

He didn't frown.

He didn't glare.

Instead, the corners of his mouth curved upwards in a slow, sensual smile.

'Always is a long time, *gummur*. We will see what you say in a week.'

Inclining his head, he turned away, effectively dismissing her, and she huffed out of the room, wishing she had the strength to slam the thick wooden door.

She didn't need a week.

She'd given him her final answer.

It wasn't her fault the high-and-mighty prince was too arrogant to accept it.

* * *

Samman waited till the door closed behind Bria before muttering a curse and flinging himself into the nearest chair.

What had he done?

After all his careful planning, all his investigations, all his meticulous research, he'd blurted his proposal like a man who'd been kicked in the head by a dozen camels.

It wasn't supposed to have happened this way.

His first mistake had been losing his head and kissing her, his second enjoying it far too much, and the last, fatal blow had come when he'd pronounced his proposal like a *fait accompli*.

He'd known a woman like Bria would appreciate a gentle lead-in to such a big decision, a clear, concise outline of what marriage to him would entail, like a finely tuned business proposal.

Instead, he'd blurted it out in the heat of the

moment, momentarily allowing passion and male pride to dominate rather than his usual coolness.

It had to stop.

He needed to give her time, time to adjust to the idea of marriage, before revealing how much he wanted her, how badly he wanted to explore the depth of feeling between them.

For he had no doubt the spark between them was real.

He had spent half a lifetime dating women, trying to find a suitable bride, but none had stimulated him on as many levels as the beautiful Bria.

And, just when he'd resigned himself to the idea of an arranged marriage to cement his dreams for Adhara's future, he'd met Bria.

His mother had been right. When love hit it was like a bolt of lightning from a thunderous Adharan sky, and since the first moment he'd laid eyes on Bria he'd been all too aware that he'd entered a tempestuous storm.

Pacing his private sitting-room, his soft-soled shoes barely making a whisper against the marble floor, he remembered the first moment he'd seen her in her casual red-and-white checked sundress with her turquoise cardigan draped across her shoulders. The colour combination should've clashed, but on her the casual clothes had added to the vibrancy which shimmered off her in seductive waves.

It had been the first thing to capture his attention at the airport—the vivid colours on the strikingly beautiful woman several car-lengths away. However, once he'd taken a curious glance, he'd been too captivated to look away, her vitality an attractive contrast to his otherwise dull trip.

In reality he shouldn't have considered her for the role of his wife. But, with his chief financial adviser's dire warnings ringing in his

ears during the twenty-four-hour plane trip
from London to Melbourne, he'd known he
would have to make a choice sooner rather than
later—and laying eyes on Bria the second after
he'd hung up had seemed like fate.

He was a firm believer in fate.

He'd already wasted countless years on a
fruitless search, when a chosen bride would've
had his country on the brink of prosperity
rather than teetering on a cliff's edge into
oblivion.

Now was the time to take a bride.

He had no other choice.

Shaking his head, he settled down to work.
However, after trying to concentrate on the cost
projections for the new city—only to find the
figures dancing like palm trees in a sandstorm
before his eyes—he gave up and poured a mint
shai, hoping the familiar tea would ease the
tension that weighed him down more than the
countless medals adorning his chest.

What had Bria thought of his uniform, his formal garb? When at home he wore nothing else. His people expected it of him, and it made him feel closer to the family he missed so much.

He'd loved sitting on his father's knee as a child, playing with the very same medals pinned on the king's chest, and had been especially happy when his mum had crouched down next to them, explaining what each of them meant: honour, loyalty, servitude, pride.

He'd loved touring the palace gardens, holding his mum's hand as she'd pointed out her favourite flowers: orange blossoms, hundreds of them, which still perfumed the air surrounding the palace to this day.

He'd loved sharing meals with them, being included in their adult discussions.

Rubbing the bridge of his nose, he closed his eyes for a moment. He'd been surrounded by love one minute, left in the hands of a demanding tyrant the next.

Not that his grandfather had been completely heartless. He'd done the best he could raising a teenager born to rule, but it just hadn't been the same as basking in his parents' love.

A fleeting image of his grandfather on his deathbed—weak, withered, yet with fire in his eyes—flashed across his mind, and he blinked, refusing to relive his grief.

Besides, he didn't need a reminder of the promise he'd made to his dead grandfather.

It was what drove him every day, what was driving him now to propose to a woman he hardly knew.

He owed it to his country.

He owed it to his family.

Winning Bria wouldn't be easy, he could see that. She was headstrong, independent and proud. She hid her emotions well, yet each time they kissed…

Even now he couldn't forget the taste of mint on her breath, the feel of her soft lips opening beneath his, responding to him, teasing him to lose his mind.

And he had for a moment.

But not any more.

He had given her a week out of courtesy, but it had been merely that—a courtesy paid to a stubborn woman.

He had no intention of taking no for an answer.

He'd make sure of it.

A knock sounded at the door and Samman glanced at his watch, knowing it had to be Hakim. His PA took punctuality very seriously.

'Your Highness.'

Hakim bowed as Samman all but yanked open the door, eager for the information he'd requested.

'Do you have what I want?'

'Of course, sir.'

Hakim handed him a plain, beige-coloured Manila folder and Samman flipped it open, even though he'd already studied these pages countless times on the flight home.

Seeing Bria's striking face staring up at him from the grainy picture on the first page slammed into him full-force again, leaving him strangely disoriented, a feeling he barely recognized, and he flipped the folder shut and threw it on a nearby table.

'Is there anything else you require, Your Highness?'

'No, that will be all, thank you.'

Hakim bowed in one fluid movement, born of years of practice, and exited the room quietly and efficiently like everything else he did.

Samman waited for the door to click shut before snapping open the folder, his gaze instantly drawn to Bria's picture again.

The photographer hadn't done her justice, yet there was no escaping the intelligence behind her golden eyes, the avid expression on her face, the slight quirk of her full lips.

The photo oozed vitality, and though of poor quality captured the essence of a woman who had snared his interest in a brief second at the airport and had held him captivated ever since.

She was the perfect choice for his bride.

If he had to take a wife in a hurry, what better choice than a woman who held him enthralled, with the possibility of everything he'd ever dreamed of developing between them?

Pleased with his decision, he scanned the rest of the information he'd long since memorised: her wealthy background, the architectural business she'd started from scratch, the harbour-side apartment in Sydney where she'd lived for the last two years, and the six months living in Chelsea, London, before that. Twenty-eight years old. No health problems.

Most importantly—and luckily for him—the last point was vital: no romantic entanglements.

He smiled the smug, self-assured smile of a
man who had been handed the perfect opportunity and intended on making the most of it.

As soon as possible.

CHAPTER SEVEN

'How did it go?'

Lou slipped off her embroidered slippers, flopped onto Bria's bed and dropped her chin in her hands, the same way she'd done countless nights at boarding school while waiting for news—or the fallout, more likely—of their latest escapade.

Bria forced a smile as she sat on the floor cross-legged, knowing she'd have to give her friend a snippet or two to assuage her curiosity, aware that full disclosure at this point wasn't an option.

'My meeting the Prince, you mean?'

Lou rolled her eyes. 'Don't play dumb with

me. You used to try that a lot at school. It didn't work then and it sure isn't going to work now. So, spill it. What did you think of him? What did you talk about?'

Bria thought he was nuts, his talk even nuttier.

Choosing her words carefully, she said, 'He's very dynamic.'

'Dynamic?' Lou wrinkled up her nose. 'What's that, a euphemism for hot? Come on, this is me you're talking to.'

Bria gnawed at her bottom lip. She'd love to come clean to her best friend and tell her the whole sorry tale: how the Prince was actually the man she'd fallen for in Melbourne, how he'd kissed her again, how he'd got some crazy idea into his head that he wanted her to marry him.

Instead, she bottled it up, just as she'd learned from a young age when coping with her father's bossiness.

'He was pleasant. We had a chat about my

stay here, his country, and his plans for the capital city. It was all very civilised.'

'Oh, is that all?'

Lou's disappointed pout piqued Bria's curiosity. Did her friend know more than she was letting on?

'What did you expect?'

Lou paused, a cheeky smile creasing her face.

'Rumour has it the Prince is after a wife. He's been dating like a madman the last few years, hence the playboy reputation. Guess I was hoping you'd be totally and utterly charmed by him, he'd sweep you off your feet, and you'd live happily ever after right here alongside me.'

Bria's heart stilled at the fairy-tale picture Lou's words depicted. However, the only truth behind her friend's words was that the Prince was after a wife.

Yes, she'd been stupid enough to be charmed by him in Melbourne, but, as for happily ever after, she'd given up that fantasy a long time ago.

'You've been reading too many of those romance novels again, haven't you?'

Lou snorted. 'Nothing wrong with a bit of romance. It's fun, something you should be having more of.'

'Don't start,' Bria said, holding up her hands to ward off her friend's usual 'you need to get out more' spiel. 'Besides, there's no way I'd consider marriage, even if he thought I was the best thing since Tim-Tams. You know how I feel about some guy thinking he has the right to order me around.'

Lou sat up and hugged her knees, wearing a rare serious expression.

'Sweetie, you know I love you, and I'm only saying this because of it, but not everyone has a relationship like your folks. You need to get past it.'

Bria stiffened, her usual reaction whenever she thought about her parents' bizarre marriage.

'I am past it,' she muttered, fiddling with the hem on her dress till she'd pleated it in tight creases.

Lou unfolded her long legs from the bed and dropped down on the Persian rug next to her.

'You're not. So what if your dad is years older than your mum? So what if he bosses her around and she panders to him? It works for them, and they're still married after all this time.'

'He's twenty-two years older. And she doesn't just pander to him, she acts like his personal lap-dog. It's degrading. He's old and obnoxious, she's gorgeous and smart, yet kowtows to him like he's a king.'

Bria snapped her fingers, wishing she could snap away every ill feeling she harboured towards her father just as easily.

'Which of course he is in Australia. Kurt Green, king of cattle barons, the richest man in the country, a real control freak who expects everyone around him to kiss his ass. I hate him.'

Lou slipped a comforting arm around her shoulders, squeezing gently, and only then did Bria ease into the gentle embrace and release some of the tension holding her rigid.

'He can't control you any more. You're free of him. You've proved yourself ten times over by going it on your own and establishing a successful business in your own right. He can't hurt you now.'

Bria sighed, wishing Lou's words were true.

However, she still heard the rumours, no matter how many incredible buildings she designed or how high she climbed the corporate ladder.

Anyone who mattered in the Australian business world still thought she was a success because of the Green name, because she was King Kurt's daughter, and it rankled. Boy, did it rankle.

'He's constantly interfering in my life in subtle ways. He still thinks he can make me do his bidding by trying to buy me off. How pathetic is that?'

'Maybe he just wants to be a part of your life?'

She froze at Lou's soft question. Kurt didn't want to be part of her life, he wanted to run it—just like he'd tried to do from the minute she'd been born.

Bria shook her head. 'Family means nothing to him. I'm a possession—a rather recalcitrant possession, that doesn't jump to his tune or behave like it should, so he sees me as some sort of challenge. No matter what I say or do he'll always try to rule me. It's his way, the only way he knows. Everyone around him does it, why not me?'

'I didn't mean to rehash unpleasant stuff for you, sweetie, but you need to realise that not every guy expects you to bow down to him.'

Suddenly, a startling image of bowing down

to a prince popped into her mind, and she mentally shoved it aside, hating how Sam's actions to date were on a par with her father's usual quest for control.

'I know,' Bria said, knowing no such thing.

Lou scuttled around to face her and grabbed both her hands.

'You think I'm mad for marrying Yusif and throwing myself into the whole royal-family bit. I saw it on your face when you first met him, I see it on your face now. You think that marrying a powerful man saps you of power, that you'd be an inferior second in the partnership, but you're wrong. Dead wrong. Yusif treats me as an equal, and I expect nothing less. Sure, I may have to behave a certain way in public and follow royal protocol, but that's a small part of our marriage—and for the joy he brings me for the rest of the time it's worth it.' Lou paused and winked. 'Worth every single step I have to lag behind him.'

'You're expected to walk behind him in public?'

Bria's hand flew to her mouth in shock, and Lou laughed as she tweaked her nose.

'Got you going for a minute, huh?'

Bria's chuckles petered out quickly as the importance of Lou's words sank in.

'Have I been that easy to see through?'

Lou nodded. 'Like glass.'

Bria squeezed her hands. 'You know how much I like Yusif, I really do, though you're probably right— I've been so caught up in my past that I lose sight of the present. Not every rich, powerful guy is like my dad, and I can see you're happy.'

'Even if my husband is away on business far too often for my liking,' Lou said, her eyes clouding for a second before she brightened. 'Though it makes the homecomings so worth it.'

Bria laughed and hugged her friend. 'Thanks

for putting up with me. And for telling me a few home truths.'

Lou pulled back, wide grin firmly in place. 'So, does this mean you'll set your sights on the Prince?'

'Hey, I didn't say I was insane!'

Besides, she didn't need to set her sights on anyone. How ironic that the Prince had his sights set on her, and she had every intention of blinding him to her.

'But you will enjoy yourself while you're here, right?'

'Of course,' Bria said, suddenly brighter than she'd been since her mind-blowing meeting with Sam.

She *was* hung up on her past and how much she loathed her father.

Time to set aside her prejudices for a while, steep herself in a new culture, and who knew? Maybe she'd have some much-needed fun in the process.

'By the way, I've been picking up a few words here and there. What does "*gummur*" mean?'

Lou's eyebrows shot up. 'Ooh, did the Prince call you that?'

It took all of Bria's negligible acting skills to keep her expression bland.

'Uh-uh. I heard Rasha saying it to one of those colourful birds in the garden this morning.'

Pretty pathetic, but all she could come up with on the spur of the moment.

'It means "my love" in Arabic. It's a literal translation of the moon, and is used to describe beautiful people. Pretty high praise around here, actually. Cute, huh?' Lou grinned. 'Boy, Rasha sure must have a thing for birds.'

Her accompanying wink told Bria she hadn't bought her poor excuse for a second, worse luck.

'Hmm.'

Bria's noncommittal response brought a burst of laughter from Lou, and she leaped off the floor, needing to distract Lou from probing any more, needing to distract herself from the disconcerting thought that Sam had called her 'his love'. Twice.

It probably didn't mean a thing.

Right?

Bria knocked twice at Sam's door, trying to still her fiddling fingers as she plucked at the fringed hem of her peasant top.

She'd been looking forward to touring the palace with Lou, but her best friend had come down with one of her blinding migraines, and from past experience Bria knew how bad they could be and how long they could last.

Unfortunately, she'd been stupid enough to open her big mouth to Rasha about missing out on the tour, and before she could blink an invitation from Sam had arrived.

Sure, she could've refused. But, considering her architectural curiosity to explore this magnificent palace was driving her nuts, not to mention the thousand and one other questions filtering through her brain, she'd accepted.

This place was nothing like she'd imagined. Where were all the bodyguards? The formality? The bowing and scraping? Apart from Sam wearing his uniform all the time, the palace seemed to function on a fairly low-key basis, surprising, considering the pomp and ceremony of royal families around the world.

The door opened as Bria raised her hand to knock again, and she made a conscious effort not to take a step back as Sam's imposing presence filled the doorway.

'I've been expecting you,' he said, smiling at her in welcome with more warmth than was warranted, considering how they'd last parted. 'Would you like some refreshments before the tour commences?'

She shook her head, wanting to get this over and done with as soon as possible.

Logically, she had no problem giving him the cold shoulder.

Physically, her heart thumped, her pulse raced and her palms grew clammy whenever he got within two feet of her.

Crazy.

'I'd like to get started,' she said, keeping her voice calm despite the shiver of anticipation that shot through her body as he nodded, stepped closer and closed the door behind him.

'As you wish.'

Bria stiffened as he moved his arm, hoping he wasn't offering her his elbow in some gentleman's gesture from days gone by. Instead, he reached into his inside jacket-pocket and pulled out a small, red leather-bound book, its yellowing pages and creased cover clearly identifying its age.

'I thought you might like this to peruse at your leisure once the tour is complete.'

'Thanks,' she said, her fingers brushing his as

he handed over the book, causing heat to scorch her cheeks, and she quickly buried her head in the pages to hide her incriminating blush.

Darn it, her body was definitely having a hard time keeping up with her brain in not reacting to the sexy prince.

'It's the history of Adhara,' she said, her embarrassment not easing up as she tried not to cringe at stating the obvious.

He nodded, amusement curving his lips into a knowing smile. Drat the man, he knew exactly how he was affecting her.

'It's an interesting insight into our culture. And it might give you a feel for what I'd like to preserve alongside the development I foresee happening over the next few years.'

Stifling a sigh of disappointment, Bria slipped the book into her pocket. She should've known there'd be more behind his kind gesture. Everything came back to his plans for his country's future and the part he hoped she'd play in them. *As if.*

'Come. We will start in the north wing.'

Thankful to escape his astute stare, she fell into step beside him, her low heels slapping against the mottled white marble and echoing through the empty corridors—the sound an instant reminder of when she'd said goodbye and walked away from him after that magical day in the rose garden back in Melbourne.

A day she had no right remembering, now that Sam had revealed his true identity, and she realised it had all been a sham, just another ploy to get what he wanted.

Quashing her annoyance with effort, she said, 'The palace is surprisingly quiet. You don't have many staff?'

'I don't spend much time here with my business interests, and see no reason to have a plethora of bored staff to wait on me hand and foot when I'm here.'

Bria quirked an eyebrow, surprised at his matter-of-fact reply. She'd assumed royalty was born to be waited on and didn't give a thought about their staff's job satisfaction or boredom levels.

'What about bodyguards? You were obviously travelling incognito in Melbourne, but what about here? Surely the monarchy would be protected at all times?'

Sam stopped at the end of a long corridor and turned left through an intricately carved archway, gesturing for her to follow.

'I have a PA, Hakim, who is also my personal bodyguard. He is highly trained. As for being protected in the palace, we are surrounded by desert as far as the eye can see. Guards are posted at the entrances, and any visitors who come within the periphery are given clearance well in advance.'

He paused outside a heavy wooden door, his hand on the door knob. 'Though it has never been a problem in Adhara. The royal family is well respected, has been since their inception. Often I travel within the city with only Hakim to accompany me. People here are respectful, with old-fashioned values.'

Bria shook her head, feeling like she'd just stepped into a time warp. For a forward-thinking modern prince, Sam seemed pretty blasé about security.

'That may be well and good, but what about rebels? Militants—terrorists? Those from outside your country who may want to do you harm?'

He smiled, the warmth in his eyes bathing her with its glow.

'Sounds like you care about me. I am flattered.'

'Don't be, I'm just curious,' she said, his nearness combined with his tender expression having a predictable effect on the blush she'd only just managed to subdue.

'In that case, let me satisfy your curiosity.'

He opened the door with a flourish and indicated she should precede him into the room.

'Adhara is a tiny independent principality, ruled by the royal family for generations. We're surrounded by wealthy sheikhdoms, and are not rich in resources, unlike our oil-rich neighbours. No one has ever wanted to invade us or steal our land, or overthrow our monarchy, and I can't see it happening now—especially as we're lagging so far behind the countries on our borders. So, you see, I am safe.'

Or content to stick your head in the sand, was Bria's first thought.

However, her mind effectively blanked as she stepped into the room, completely overwhelmed by its sheer beauty, the French Provincial theme in complete contrast to the Arabic designs in the rest of the palace.

The Louis XV-style furniture—with its curves and carved motifs, the exquisite chinoiserie inlays, the richness of the fabrics, the asymmetrical edge of the scalloped sideboard, and the rounded, almost sensual shape of the cabriole legs on the chairs—had her eyes darting every which way, absorbing the striking period pieces and how they combined in a welcoming atmosphere of relaxed elegance.

'Not what you expected?'

'It's incredible,' she said softly, amazed at the cosiness of the room in comparison with the gargantuan proportions of the rest of the palace, drawn in by its comforting warmth.

'I agree.'

She raised her eyes to his, surprised by the glitter of emotion, of pride, as if he were more than pleased by her reaction.

'This room was my mother's private sitting-room. When she wasn't by my father's side she spent many hours here, reading, answering correspondence, relaxing.'

Sam's low voice lulled her; his tone was

almost reverent, and she stared at the man she'd thought she knew, ashamed to admit she didn't know him at all.

She'd labelled him a liar, a fraud, a powerful man who used his status to manipulate those around him. Yet right now, in this shared moment, she glimpsed a deeper side to him, a side which drew her despite her intention to keep her distance.

'Tell me about your family,' she said softly, unwilling to break the intimate spell cast upon them as soon as they'd stepped into this enchanting room.

Indicating she should take a seat, he chose a Louis XV chair opposite her.

'My father was a great ruler, and my mother stood by him every step of the way. She was French, the daughter of an ambassador. They met in Paris and married within a year.'

Bria's jaw dropped as the implications of what he'd just said sunk in.

'Theirs was a love match? And your mother wasn't royalty?'

Sam smiled, all the love and affection he felt for his parents evident in that one simple gesture.

'No, she wasn't. But my father loved her, she loved him, and that love sustained them through everything they faced together.'

Bria couldn't comprehend a love like that, let alone imagine it. There was no love in her parents' marriage, at least, not the overwhelming emotion Sam was describing.

'What happened?'

A cloud of sadness passed over his face.

'They died in a plane crash when I was ten. My grandfather raised me after that.'

An apology would have sounded too trite after the depth of emotion she'd just seen in his eyes, so she settled for, 'You must miss them.'

He nodded, his sorrow almost palpable.

'We were a very close family. My parents never hid the fact of how much they loved me. My childhood was special.'

Bria managed an understanding smile, while inside her heart ached.

What would he think of her childhood?

The strict rules she'd lived by—like 'kids are to be seen only occasionally and never heard'—her father's impossible, rigid structure for a child to follow, the cold-hearted nannies who had watched her eat every green vegetable off her plate with eagle eyes as her parents had dined alone—while the hours she'd actually spent with her parents each year could be counted on her fingers and toes.

If Sam's childhood had been special, hers had been hell—cold, frosty silences punctuated by barked orders from a heartless father who controlled everyone around him, and an insipid mother who pandered to his every whim.

'Bria? I'm sorry if my memories have made you sad.'

She shook her head and reached across the space dividing them to lay a comforting hand on his.

'Your memories are priceless. I was just thinking how lucky you are.'

'Yes. Lucky,' he said, turning his hand over to capture hers, his potent gaze never leaving hers for an instant.

Her heart picked up tempo as silence stretched between them, but rather than feel uncomfortable she could've sat in this cosy room holding hands with this man for ever.

'Why did you share your family memories with me? Why did you bring me here?'

She finally broke the silence when her heart expanded and filled with an emotion she couldn't acknowledge, let alone contemplate.

'Because I want to re-establish the bond we had in Melbourne. I want you to see I am not the ogre you think I am. But most of all I want you to understand there's more to me than this.'

He gestured towards his uniform with his free hand before waving it around the room. 'And this. Yes, this room holds special memories for me, but it's just that—a room, part of the palace. It's not who I am or a part of the real me.'

He moved with the speed of a panther as he sat next to her without releasing her hand. 'The real me is the man you learned to like in Melbourne, the man without the encumbrances of a crown or the expectations of a country on his shoulders. Do you see him?'

For a horrifying second the unexpected sting of tears burned the back of her eyes, and Bria blinked, startled by Sam's blunt honesty, hating how vulnerable he made her feel by forcing her to acknowledge there was more to him than a crown.

'Do you?'

Sam tilted her chin up with his other hand, forcing her to meet his direct stare, to see the flicker of uncertainty in its dark depths.

He had opened up in the last few minutes, giving her a glimpse into the man behind the title, and as much as she wanted to admit how appealing that was she couldn't do it. Her defence mechanisms were too ingrained, too entrenched, for her to take a chance now on something she didn't understand.

Taking a steadying breath, she said, 'I see a man who would do anything for his country. A man with responsibilities. A man who would like me to fall in with his plans whatever it takes.'

Her answer disappointed him.

She could see it in his eyes, in the clenching of his jaw, the swiftness in which he released her.

'You are wrong about me, Bria Green, and I have every intention of showing you the real me over the next week.'

While Bria's heart raced with uncharacteristic fervour, she managed a weak smile at the thought.

CHAPTER EIGHT

BRIA had been warned.

Sam had made it more than clear he intended on showing her the 'real him' over the next week, and after their tour of the palace had concluded yesterday, and she'd had time to distance herself from the memory of his mother's sitting room and what had taken place there, she'd rationalised the whole thing.

His Highness could try and impress her all he liked by showing her his human side, it didn't mean she had to succumb to his charms.

So, when he'd offered to take her into Adhara City for her first trip into his country's capital, she'd accepted, safe in the logic that the Prince could try to schmooze her all he liked but it wouldn't do him an ounce of good. She was prepared for whatever he had to dish out.

However, that didn't stop her pulse pounding when she climbed into the front seat of the four-wheel drive and Sam slid behind the wheel.

'You're driving?'

'Yes. Hakim has some other business to take care of later. He will follow behind us and keep watch from a discreet distance while we're in the city. Is there a problem?'

'No, not at all,' she said, fixing a too-bright smile on her face before staring out of the side window, anything to distract herself from noticing how incredibly handsome he looked in his uniform.

He'd been impressive enough in the designer suits he'd favoured in Melbourne, but there was something about the man in uniform—an added air of authority, of superiority—which he didn't have without it.

'Good. The mosaics you are interested in for your client are on the outskirts of the capital, so I thought we could look at them first then drive through Adhara City afterwards. It would give you an opportunity to see some of the early development.'

Bria refrained from snorting—just.

'Give me an opportunity to fall in line with your plan, you mean? Show me the city, dazzle me with a little PR, and hope I jump at your crazy scheme?'

Sam didn't take his eyes from the dusty road, though his fingers clenched the steering wheel tighter.

'I can assure you that marriage to me would not be crazy,' he said, his voice low, tight, controlled, its husky timbre in stark contrast to his tense posture.

She'd insulted him.

A man of his status, with hordes obeying his every whim, wouldn't be used to refusal let alone someone flinging his proposal back in his face.

Embarrassed by how churlish she'd sounded, she said, 'I'm sorry. I didn't mean to ridicule you. It's just that I'm having a hard time absorbing all this.'

His hands relaxed on the steering wheel, and he shot her a glance bordering on tender.

'Let us be friends, enjoy each other's company, and leave any decisions till the end of the week. Is that so difficult?'

Was it ever! It was hard enough holding him at arm's length when she despised him for wanting to possess her like a chattel, how would she fare if she actually grew to like him?

More than you do all ready?

Ignoring her inner voice—the same voice which had deserted her in Melbourne, when she'd gone ahead and let down her guard around him against her better judgement—she said, 'I'll try, but I'm not making any promises.'

'That is all I ask.'

They lapsed into silence, and Bria sank against the soft leather seat, grateful for whatever reprieve she got from making conversation with him.

She hadn't slept much last night. Her head had filled with snippets from their tour together, the insights he'd given her into his personality, his family. Forcing polite small talk was a big ask, considering it was difficult to be anywhere near this man while her thoughts wandered all over the place.

For that was exactly what they were doing: wandering, vacillating, vague and wishy-washy, when she'd been so sure of herself about refusing his proposal.

Yet somehow in the wee small hours, in the half-wake, half-dream state when she did some of her best thinking for work, she'd imagined herself by Sam's side.

As his wife. Princess Bria.

Crazy.

Ludicrous.

So not going to happen.

But for one, tiny second she'd been struck by how secure the thought had made her feel, a totally foreign feeling for a woman who'd spent a lifetime forging her independence and relishing it.

'We're almost there.'

Bria jumped, drawn back to the present by the dulcet tones of the man who'd featured in her outlandish happily-ever-after scenario earlier that morning, and wishing she hadn't pictured the two of them together for longer than the next few weeks.

'You are mainly after mosaics?'

'Yes, that's why I came to Adhara. Ned Wilson is my biggest client, and he wants his new house to be perfect.'

'The patterns on the outskirts of the city are ex-quisite. You should find something suitable to satisfy the most discerning client. And while we're here you can check out the prime land where I envisage further housing developments.'

She heard the pride in his voice, and wondered what else this self-professed modern prince envisaged for his country's future.

'What are your other plans for the city?'

He pulled over in front of a demarcated block of land set on high ground, with commanding views of the small city laid like toy blocks beneath them, and switched off the engine.

'This city is going to make Adhara a prosperous country.'

His gaze never left the tiny sandstone buildings in the distance, which were scattered in haphazard disarray along winding streets with little sense of direction, as he made a sweeping gesture with his hand.

'I want Adhara City to rival major cities like Dubai for development, for tourism, for world recognition.'

Bria followed his gaze, trying to see his vision and failing.

Rival Dubai, the star city of the United Arab Emirates? That would take years of planning, of infrastructure, of design, of building…

And, just like that, a frisson of anticipation shot through her, jolting her out of the semi-lethargy which had pervaded her tired body on the short drive here.

What would it be like to design an entire city, a showpiece city, the capital city of a country?

A buzz started deep in her brain like a thousand bees in a hive, and she closed her eyes, briefly imagining the various heights of new buildings, the domed shapes to blend with the environment, the raw materials needed to enhance the landscape's beauty yet stand out anyway.

'You can see it, can't you?'

Her eyes snapped open and she slowly turned to face Sam, knowing her face would give her away even if she tried to lie to him.

'It would certainly be a challenge,' she said, her gut churning with excitement at the feverish glint in his eyes.

'It would be all yours.'

He shrugged and turned away, refocussing his attention on the view as she struggled to dampen her creative juices.

Unfortunately it didn't work, and she found her gaze drawn back to the city, lightning-fast pictures already forming in her mind as her fingers itched for pencil and paper.

She didn't want to ask the next logical question, she really didn't, but there was no denying her business brain once it had engaged.

'The finances on a project this large would be astronomical. Do you have a budget in place?'

He hesitated before answering, and she sensed a definite chill in the air as he turned to face her, his expression glacial.

'The finances are under control. Investors are

in place. Once we have the right person for the job, it will be business as usual.'

'Right,' she said, confused by his sudden coldness. 'And you think I'm the right person, huh?'

'I don't think, I know.'

He pronounced it like a foregone conclusion, like every other outrageous statement he'd made to her since she'd arrived, as if he had the absolute and final word.

Well, she had news for him.

However before she could set him straight he stepped from the car and walked round to the passenger side in record time, opening her door before she could do it herself.

'Come. We will inspect the land, see if you have any ideas for my country's future.'

Bria bit her tongue, wondering if he was trying to alienate her on purpose.

First the brush-off after she'd questioned the city's finances, as if women shouldn't bother their heads about such matters, and now the deliberate emphasis on her ideas for the city when she hadn't agreed to his proposal.

If she didn't know any better, she'd say the arrogant prince was rattled about something. But what?

As Bria stepped from the car and onto the chrome sideboard, her low-heeled sandal caught, and she stumbled, pitching headfirst towards the dirt. Sam caught her in a split second, his strong arms steadying her, holding her way too close and way too tight.

'Thanks,' she murmured, trapped less than a foot away from his chest, her hands braced against cool cotton, while his underlying heat radiated through his dress shirt and burned her palms.

'My pleasure.'

Something in his voice drew her gaze slowly upwards till it connected with his—dark, unreadable, mysterious—and she swallowed, unprepared for the swift surge of longing to close the short gap between them and bury her face into his chest.

She could smell him, the faintest trace of sandalwood tickling her nose, teasing her senses, and her body responded on a visceral level, her belly flip-flopping as she remembered all too clearly the other times she'd got this close to him.

Move! her brain commanded.

Relax, her body responded.

'If you are all right, we can inspect the site.'

Sam's voice broke the seductive spell which seemed to envelop her whenever she got near him, and she pulled away, shaken by her physical reaction to a man she had no intention of getting closer to despite her traitorous body.

'I'm fine. Let's get on with it,' she said, stalking towards the barren acres of pegged land as fast as her feet could carry her, heat flooding her cheeks as she tried to ignore Sam's smug laugh.

* * *

'I've never seen anything like it. It's en-chanting.'

Something thudded painfully in Samman's chest, something he'd never felt before, as Bria gripped his arm and pointed at the *souk* in front of them.

Her eyes glittered with excitement, and his chest contracted, expanded and made breath-ing altogether difficult at her natural reaction to a common marketplace.

'We have several *souks*,' he said, desperately trying to ignore the desire snaking through his body at her innocuous touch. 'Apart from this one, we have a spice *souk* also.'

'Whatever development occurs, you must keep these. They are part of the city's natural charm.'

'I agree,' he said, his gaze drawn to her face, her beautiful skin the colour of buttermilk, her unique honey eyes, her sensual mouth…

He loved this city, but right now the only

natural charm he could focus on was standing right in front of him with happiness etched across her exquisite features.

She withdrew her hand quickly, a slight blush staining her cheeks, and he hid a triumphant smile.

Oh, yes, she felt the spark between them, even if she didn't want to acknowledge it.

He may want to take things slow for her sake, but that didn't stop him wanting this mesmerising woman with a ferocity that scared him. And little if anything in this world scared him.

'Do we have time to take a stroll through the market?'

'Of course.'

He would do everything to show off his city, to convince her that she must stay, become his wife and let him set his plans in motion.

He hadn't wanted to lie to her about any of this, but she'd come too close to guessing the truth in the car when she'd probed about his finances, and he couldn't risk alienating her further—not when his objective was clear, close and obtainable.

'Come. I will show you our *souk*.'

He offered her his elbow, sure she'd refuse, but to his surprise and joy she only hesitated a moment before slipping her hand through it, her light touch doing little to dampen his latent libido.

They strolled between the many stalls, her gasps of delight, combined with the occasional excited squeeze on his arm, surprising him.

He'd hoped she'd enjoy her first visit to the city, had hoped she'd be as enthralled with it as he was, but he'd never expected such an open, honest reaction.

It gave him hope, hope for a future he'd envisaged since that fateful day by his grandfather's bedside three years ago.

'Wow,' she said, releasing his arm as she stopped dead in her tracks, her wide-eyed gaze darting between the countless, dazzling gold stalls in front of them.

He laughed. 'I see you are a true woman.'

She didn't bristle as he'd expected. Instead, her rueful smile warmed his heart.

'What woman doesn't like jewellery?'

'I see you don't wear much.'

He picked up her right hand, studying the simple opal on the ring finger with curiosity, wondering if the man she'd lived with in London had given it to her and, if so, how much it meant.

Hakim's investigations had been thorough; there had been no contact between her and Ellis Finley since the lease on their flat had expired two years ago, but one never knew with women. Their actions didn't always correspond with what was in their hearts.

'Is this ring of special significance?'

Her gaze followed his to the oval opal set in white gold, the stone's emerald, sapphire and ruby depths catching the filtered sunlight through the *souk*'s shade sails.

'I bought it for myself, a graduation present.'

He nodded, relieved it wasn't a sentimental trinket from an ex-lover.

'Did you not have anyone else to buy you a graduation gift? Your parents, perhaps?'

She practically snatched her hand out of his, and wrapped her arms around her middle as if warding him off. 'My parents gave me a diamond tennis-bracelet from Tiffany for my graduation.'

Her cold, clipped tones left him with little doubt as to what she'd thought of that particular gift.

'You do not get along with them?'

Her lips compressed into a thin, hard line before she spoke. 'My father wants to control everything, and everyone. My mother agrees with anything he says. We don't see eye to eye.'

'This does not sound like a simple misunder-standing.'

She shook her head, her gold-streaked hair tumbling about her face, and begging him to smooth it back.

'No, there is nothing simple about it. I don't get along with my dad—never have, never will. He takes the art of manipulation and control to new heights, like that stunt he pulled in Melbourne by organising me a limo, when he knows I hated using them as a kid. He's still trying to get me to jump to his tune, and I won't have a bar of it. We rarely speak any more.'

'I am sorry,' he said, saddened that a bright, intelligent woman like her could not see the value of family, no matter how many faults they appeared to have.

For him, family was everything: the love, the warmth, the support. He craved it like a thirsty traveller in the desert—which is exactly why he'd showed her his mother's sitting room yesterday, why he'd told her about the love his parents had shared.

With a little luck, they could have the same.

'Don't be sorry,' she said, waving away his concern with a flick of her wrist. 'Speaking of family, you told me about your grandfather raising you after your parents died. Does that mean you were a prince since the age of ten?'

He nodded, proud of who he was, of what he'd been born to do.

'My grandfather groomed me all those years, prepared me for my rightful role. He insisted I studied at Oxford and lived my life before taking over the day-to-day running of the country.'

'That's some responsibility for a child to bear,' she said, a thoughtful expression on her face as she studied him with curious eyes. 'I guess we both didn't have much time to be children, by the sound of it.'

He shrugged. 'It did not matter to me. This is what I was born to do. It is my destiny.'

She smiled, the simple action transforming her face from beautiful to stunning in an instant.

'You're pretty hooked on all that stuff, aren't you? First it was fate in Melbourne, now destiny. Next you'll be telling me this is written in the stars.'

'This?'

He knew exactly what she referred to, but he wanted to hear her say it, to see if she was as unaffected by the attraction between them as she'd like him to believe.

'This,' she said, her hand fluttering between them like a delicate bird, the amber flecks in her eyes glowing like the priceless gold surrounding them.

He captured her hand and raised it to his lips, placing a slow, lingering kiss on the soft skin of her palm, before enclosing her fingers over it.

'You will see how destiny works, *gummur*, then you will believe.'

When her lips parted in a small, shocked O, he turned away and indicated they head for the nearest exit, determined to keep his feelings for this woman under control for now—no matter how much his heart wanted to do otherwise.

CHAPTER NINE

BRIA closed her eyes, wriggled her toes and sighed in ecstasy as a cascade of warm water poured over her feet.

She might not have felt entirely comfortable, having Rasha assigned as her personal maid to be ordered about at will, but right now her principles dissolved as quickly as the citrus oil in the foot bath as her feet throbbed and begged for attention.

'Rasha, you are a miracle worker,' she said, almost passing out in bliss as the young woman's firm hands kneaded her aching feet with the skill of a reflexologist twice her age.

Rasha giggled and continued her ministrations. 'You should not wear such footwear for long walks. It is not healthy.'

Bria nodded, not willing to acknowledge she hadn't expected to walk so far today or to enjoy herself so much.

But she couldn't think about that now, not when the memory of Sam's kiss still burned like a brand on her palm.

'You should come shopping with me, let me select some clothes and shoes for you. Much more comfortable,' Rasha said, pushing Bria's insteps with firm pressure.

'You're probably right,' Bria said, opening her eyes as an image of herself dressed like a harem girl popped into her head, the glimmer of an idea blossoming as quickly as her unwelcome feelings for the Prince.

So Sam thought he could toy with her— present a marriage proposal like a business plan, complete with fringe benefits, yet continue to confuse her with his loaded glances and impulsive actions and implications of something more between them?

What did he really want from her?

She'd never trusted easily, and something about this whole bizarre scenario niggled—the playboy prince suddenly needed a wife, and it just so happened he'd set his sights on her?

Uh-uh. She didn't buy it, not for a second.

Maybe it was time to turn the tables on His Secretive Highness and see what he would do.

'Actually, that's a brilliant idea. Maybe you'll accompany me tomorrow?'

Rasha beamed. 'It will be my pleasure. Now, I will leave your feet to soak for ten minutes before returning. Is this suitable?'

'You're amazing, Rasha, and I can't thank you enough for all this.'

Rasha blushed, executed a funny little bow, and left the room while Bria shook her head in amazement, wondering if she'd wake up any moment and find this was all a dream.

After an enlightening day in more ways than one she'd come back to her room with every muscle in her feet screaming, courtesy of the miles she'd walked in low-heeled sandals, only to find the drapes drawn, candles lit and a warm foot-bath complete with floating lemon slices and frangipani petals.

The fresh citrus-and-floral fragrance had hung heavy in the air, welcoming, intoxicating, and she'd barely raised a protest when Rasha had insisted on giving her a foot massage.

Now she could barely move, let alone walk, and she settled back into the comfy sofa, her feet soothed by the warm water, her mind a mess of swirling thoughts and supposition.

Adhara City was beautiful, almost primitive in some aspects, startlingly modern in others, but with limitless potential. An architect's dream, and she'd practically buzzed with excitement during the entire tour.

Though that could've had something to do

with the sexy prince by her side at all times, his presence a constant reminder of the kind of foolishness she could consider, given half a chance.

He wanted her for his wife, in every sense of the word, and what would she get in return?

Something he didn't even know she wanted: recognition for her work which didn't depend on the Green name, recognition worldwide by people who didn't know Kurt Green and all he stood for.

She had to admit it was tempting, and now that she'd seen the city for herself…

No, she couldn't consider it.

But it's sound business.

No, she couldn't do it.

But it could set you free once and for all.

Yeah, but at what cost?

To be free from the burden of being a Green only to find herself trapped in a loveless marriage to an all-controlling man—wasn't that the type of relationship of her nightmares?

'This is pointless,' she muttered, trying to relax her feet when she realised she'd tensed up, paddling them around, and in doing so splashing water all over the marble tiles.

She'd never agree to his crazy proposal. But that didn't mean she couldn't have a little fun, right?

Sam might talk about business propositions, yet she knew he felt the same attraction she did. Apart from him expecting full intimacies if they married, it was written all over his face whenever they got close; his desire was clearly visible in his eyes when they touched. He'd already intimated as much with his determination to get her to recognise the 'real him'.

So, the Prince wanted a wife?

Well, she might not be able to give him exactly what he wanted, but it would be fun to give him a shake-up along the way.

'You are missing Miss Eloise, yes?'

Bria looked up from the fine chiffon scarf

flowing like liquid silk through her fingers and smiled.

'She's only gone for a few days. And I think her husband was missing her more.'

Rasha's eyes misted over, while Bria wondered what it would be like to be that young, that innocent, and still believe in romance.

'They are a lovely couple. Perhaps you will find a husband while you are here?'

Bria stifled a cough, settling for clearing her throat instead. 'I am not looking for a husband.'

'But perhaps a husband will come looking for you.'

Bria's gaze snapped up, searching Rasha's face for any hidden meaning behind her innocuous words. However, the young girl appeared as guileless as ever, and Bria shrugged, needing a change of topic fast.

'I don't have time for a husband. Now, how do I say "how much is this?"?'

'Bekaam hada?'

'Thanks.'

Bria turned to the shopkeeper, a wizened old woman swathed in head-to-toe black, and let the new phrase roll off her tongue.

The shopkeeper's instant grin warmed her heart and, though she couldn't understand a word of her fast response, Bria soon joined in the spirit of haggling, with Rasha acting as interpreter.

Three outfits, four silk scarves, two pairs of butter-soft leather sandals and a pair of embroidered slippers later, Bria thanked the shopkeeper and followed Rasha into the scorching midday Adhara sun.

'You drive a hard bargain,' Bria said, rattling her bags in Rasha's direction and chuckling. *'Shokrun.'*

'El'afou tekram,' Rasha said, propelling her towards the car before she could say anything else.

Confused, Bria said, 'I'm assuming you just

said "you are welcome" in response to my thank-you?'

'Yes, yes, you are picking up Arabic very quickly, but we must hurry now.'

'Why?'

Rasha bundled her into the back seat of the four-wheel drive, slid in beside her and fired off rapid instructions to the driver before answering her.

'You are having dinner with the Prince tonight. You must prepare.'

'But that won't take me all afternoon.'

In fact, she'd counted on a few more hours of retail therapy to keep her mind off the fact she'd agreed to have dinner with Sam.

Sure, she wanted to give him a bit of a shake-up, but, the more she thought about it, maybe it wasn't such a good idea.

Each time she was with Sam something happened. A look, a touch, a feeling that no matter how cool she tried to play it there was no denying the underlying current buzzing between them.

'Surely you want to look your best for an evening with the most powerful man in the country?'

Rasha's puzzled frown lasted but a second as the young woman suddenly grinned. 'Ah, you are nervous. Do not worry, I will make you very *gameelah* for the Prince.'

'I hope that means pretty,' Bria mumbled, shaking her head at the thought of tizzying up for Sam.

It wasn't like she had to impress the guy or anything. He already wanted to marry her.

'You will be beautiful.' Rasha snapped her fingers. 'Who knows, maybe the Prince can help you find a husband.'

'Who knows?' Bria echoed, turning away to hide a sudden smile at the irony of the situation.

She didn't need any help in that department.

In fact, fending off the Prince himself would take all her cunning and resourcefulness.

Luckily for her, she'd always been resourceful.

However several hours later, after begging off Rasha's offer to do her hair and help her dress, she stood before the full-length mirror in her room, knowing there was a huge difference between teasing Sam into admitting there was more behind his proposal and being able to handle that knowledge herself.

She'd wanted to startle him tonight.

If her appearance was anything to go by, she should achieve that goal with flying colours.

Bria could barely recognise herself in the flowing pale gold *salwaar kameez*, the wide-leg trousers elongating her legs to improbable proportions, and the long-sleeved tunic somehow managing to accentuate her body rather than hide it.

Her hair wasn't responding well to Adhara's

dry heat, so she'd ditched any styling product and piled the lot on top of her head in casual disarray. However, rather than looking messy, the up-do accentuated the care she'd taken with her make-up.

She'd aimed for casual Middle Eastern chic—to her critical eyes, she'd somehow morphed into an exotic princess.

Cringing at her inadvertent comparison, she turned away from the mirror and slid her feet into a new pair of gold sandals.

She wanted to make Sam sit up and take notice.

Well, time to see if the Prince had more on his mind than business.

And time to find out exactly what it was.

'Welcome to the Prince's private dining room,' Hakim said, opening the door with a flourish to Bria's tentative knock. 'He is waiting for you.'

'Thanks,' she said, her tummy tumbling with

nervous anticipation as she stepped into a room taken straight from *Arabian Nights*.

'Enjoy your meal.'

Hakim bowed and stepped out of the room, closing the door softly, leaving her trying not to gawk at her surroundings.

Everything was done in the palest shades of green, from the ice-mint walls to the tiny mosaic tiles framing the traditional dome-shaped windows, from the low-lying sofas to the marble tiles. It had a cooling effect, like stepping into the lushest rainforest, and she moved further into the room, tilting her head back to absorb the impact of the ceiling.

'Beautiful.'

Her head snapped back, barely giving her enough time to absorb the hand-painted mural of a dusk sky with a sprinkling of early stars scattered like diamonds across mauve silk.

However, Sam wasn't talking about the ceiling.

She could see it in every tense line of his body, from his rigid shoulders to his clenched fists, in the admiration shining clearly from his eyes. She smiled, empowered by the thought that she could set him on edge this much.

'This *room* is beautiful,' she said, wondering if he'd pick her up on the clarification.

He inclined his head, as if agreeing with her, though his mesmerising coal-black eyes never left her face for an instant as he crossed the room to stand in front of her.

'You are right. The room is beautiful. You are exquisite.'

Her heart fluttered like a caged bird as he picked up her hand and placed a barely-there kiss on the back of it.

The kiss was nothing like the heated, erotic kiss he'd pressed on her palm at the market yesterday—but the mere touch of his lips anywhere near her skin set off a chain reaction within her body as nerve endings hotwired, her skin tingled and her pulse skittered out of control.

'Did you choose that outfit especially for me?'

'I dress for myself, not to impress any man.'

His mouth kicked up in a cynical smile that said he didn't believe her for a second.

'But I'm not just any man, am I?'

'No, you're more conceited than most,' she said, snatching her hand out of his, but softening the abrupt action with a coy little smile of her own, enjoying their sparring.

He laughed, a low, rumbling sound which rolled over her in an intoxicating wave.

'You have some very strong opinions. Perhaps we can debate them further over dinner.'

'I'm up for it if you are,' she said, throwing down a challenge she knew he'd accept.

Powerful men like Sam never backed down. He'd push her no matter how gallant his intentions to wait a week for her answer to his proposal. And she knew this intimate dinner for two was just another part of some elaborate plan on his part to convince her to accept.

Well, let him push.

She had a few games of her own to play with the gallant prince, including discovering his real motivation behind wanting her for his wife.

'As you wish.'

He gestured for her to step before him, and she moved into another room. It was smaller this time but just as grandiose, with its ornate filigree wrought-iron carvings framing the windows, chiffon-thin curtains in ivory, and another stunning ceiling-mural depicting dusk.

Sighing, she stepped into the room, knowing that no matter what happened over the next few weeks, leaving all this beauty behind was going to be tough.

'I have requested a simple meal for us tonight. Please, let us begin.'

Sam held out her chair and she sat, the

faintest waft of sandalwood drifting over her as he moved away, and she knew it wasn't only the beautiful designs of the Prince's rooms she would miss.

'Thanks. You've gone to a lot of trouble,' she said, admiring the formal table-setting with shining silver, crystal glasses and several domed dishes set in front of them.

'We have to eat.'

He shrugged, as if uncomfortable with her praise and gestured for her to serve.

'We have goat *pilau*, spiced-mutton chops on couscous, and grilled vegetables. Please, eat.'

Though her stomach churned with nerves, she managed to help herself to a portion of each dish, the tantalising aromas making her mouth water.

'Mmm…this is good,' she murmured, forking *pilau* into her mouth and savouring the highly spiced rice. 'You have a wonderful cook.'

He nodded, apparently pleased by her response to the food. 'Whenever I travel I look forward to returning to one of Zizi's meals.'

'Do you travel often?'

'Whenever business demands it.'

'By the extent of your current plans for development, I'd guess that would be often?'

He laid down his cutlery and fixed her with a piercing glare.

'Why the sudden interest in my business? Is there something you want to tell me? An answer you want to give me?'

Bria silently cursed; her plan to pump him for information had backfired so quickly.

'I was being polite.'

'Dinner companions making small talk? Is that all?'

'Of course. What else could it be?'

She dipped her gaze to her plate and attacked her food with renewed vigour.

She already knew Sam was smart, so she'd

just have to be a tad more subtle on her quest for information.

Spearing a piece of mutton with her fork, she couldn't help but think back to their first dinner together and how different this was. Back then she'd been on her guard, determined to hold a sexy man at bay despite an overwhelming attraction.

Now, though the attraction still sizzled between them, he was the one on guard, and if she wanted to discover his real motivation for proposing to her she'd need to tread carefully.

Thankfully, the rest of the dinner passed easily as they stuck to safe topics like the weather, the markets she'd visited, and the mosaics she'd discovered.

However, as they lingered over fresh figs served with yoghurt and honey, her curiosity got the better of her and she tried a different tack.

'You're a busy man. You mentioned yesterday that your grandfather groomed you to take on the role of prince—I'm surprised he didn't arrange your marriage also.'

Sam stiffened and pushed his chair back from the table. 'He tried.'

'What happened?'

'We fought. Often.'

'I'm sorry,' she said, searching his carefully blanked face for a clue to his feelings.

'Don't be. My grandfather and I had a fairly solid relationship. We just didn't see eye to eye on the subject of a suitable bride.'

Suddenly, a thought wended its way into her head, and once there refused to budge.

'You loved someone, didn't you? And your grandfather didn't approve. Is that why you want to marry me—to ensure it's only a business arrangement and there are no feelings involved?'

It made perfect sense, and his quick look-away glance confirmed her suspicion.

'There has been no one special.'

His cold, flat voice raised goosebumps on

her skin, and she surreptitiously rubbed her arms beneath the table.

He must've loved this mystery woman very much for him to have shut down so completely, and for a fleeting moment something akin to jealousy stabbed her.

What would it be like to be loved by a man like Sam?

To be wanted, truly wanted, for herself, and not for her business acumen or her body?

Sadly, she'd never find out.

'Let us take coffee in the other room,' he said, pulling out her chair and effectively ending the conversation.

So much for teasing him a little and getting to the bottom of why he'd really proposed to her.

She'd wanted answers tonight; it looked like she'd got them.

But at what cost?

Right now she'd alienated Sam without meaning to, and judging by his stiff posture and stilted movements she'd have to do some fast work to make amends.

'I'd like to take a trip out to the desert tomorrow,' she said, smiling her thanks for the small cup of strong coffee he handed her.

Thankfully, his frown disappeared as he chose the seat opposite her.

'Excellent. I was going to make a similar suggestion. Of course I will accompany you, give you a tour of my land. It is refreshing, seeing my country through your eyes.'

She should've been offended by his high-handedness; 'of course I will accompany you'— yet another indication of a man who didn't doubt he was in control for a second. However, he'd tempered his assumption with the veiled compliment that he enjoyed her reaction to Adhara.

Besides, what she'd seen of this exotic country had fuelled her curiosity, and what better way to learn more than with the ruler of the land himself?

'Thanks for the offer. I want to get a feel for the land. It's something I do when I take on any job.'

For a moment his eyes glittered with triumph, and she bit her tongue, belatedly realising her response sounded like she was accepting his proposal rather than gaining expertise to design a client's house.

'Fine. It is settled, then. We will leave early, before the heat is too fierce.'

'Great,' she said, thankful he'd lost the frown brought on by talk of his old girl-friends, nervous that it had been replaced by a speculative gleam in the chocolate depths of his eyes.

'Bria?'

'Yes?'

'I will make sure your first trip to the desert is one you will never forget.'

She managed a tight smile as her heart thudded against her rib cage, willing herself to believe he didn't mean anything by his smooth words, while a small part of her couldn't wait to see what he had in store.

CHAPTER TEN

IT HAD not been Samman's intention to take Bria to the Oasis.

However, the minute he'd sat behind the wheel this morning and had been assailed by her fresh fragrance—the faintest hint of the citrus soap guests used mingled with her own unique scent—he hadn't been thinking clearly.

He'd fielded all her enthusiastic questions, had swelled with pride at her genuine response to his land's beauty, and it had seemed only natural to bring her here.

Now, as he turned off the engine and turned to find her quizzical amber gaze on him, he knew he shouldn't have brought her.

This was his sanctuary.

No one came here.

Ever.

'What is this place?'

He gripped the wheel, knowing he couldn't drive away without appearing insane, all too aware he couldn't lie to her either. She would ask someone at the residence, make some remark about this place, and he'd rather not have his private business bandied about among his staff.

'It is called the Oasis.'

'It's beautiful,' she said, admiration clearly audible, and he turned to look at her, his heart clenching at the look of awe on her face.

He cleared his throat. 'Come. You must see all of it.'

Her startled gaze flew to his as he silently cursed his gruff tone.

He was no good at this—hiding his feelings, holding back his emotions.

There was no question he had to give Bria

time, but with every second he spent in her company, the further she drew him under her spell, the more he wanted her.

Quite simply, she captivated him.

He'd never met anyone like her, and he'd convince her to agree to his marriage proposal if it killed him.

'After you.'

He opened the passenger door and waited for her to alight, willing himself not to reach out and tuck a stray strand of hair behind her ear as she stepped to the ground. Her hair shimmered like gold in the harsh Adharan sun, beckoning him to touch it, to see if it felt as silky soft as it appeared, and he clenched his fist to stop from reaching out.

'Lead the way,' she said, staring at him with a quirked eyebrow as if she couldn't figure him out.

Which was just as well, for if she knew what was going through his mind at that moment, how much he wanted her, she'd bolt quicker than his prized thoroughbred-stallion.

The longer he spent in this stunning woman's company, he knew it would be easier to trek without water through his beloved desert than give her up. Though he knew it was too soon to bring her here, he ignored the niggle of doubt and ushered her through the small stone-walled compound and into the house beyond.

A hut, really, with its rough-hewn, sandy stone walls and crude furniture. He liked it this way—without adornment, without pretension.

It had been his hideaway since his youth, a refuge where he'd come to think, to relax, and later to grieve.

Though his grandfather had been callous at times, he'd understood the need for solitude, the need to escape from having his every move under constant scrutiny, and had shown Samman this place, had given him this gift.

And now Samman was sharing it with Bria.

He felt too raw here, too exposed, as if by bringing her here she would see too much.

Perhaps that was what he wanted—to reveal a little more of himself, as he'd done in showing her his mother's sitting room.

Despite her reticence at admitting the depth of feeling between them, the more time they spent together the closer they grew. He could feel it. If only she would too.

Now he'd opened up his heart a tad more. Was he being too foolish? Too impulsive?

But it was too late.

It was done, and he'd have to suffer the consequences if she didn't understand how he felt about this place or, worse, saw right into his soul at the truth buried there.

'Oh, Sam, it's breathtaking.'

Her gasp of delight banished his worries as he joined her at a rear window.

'This is the reason it is called the Oasis,' he said, overcome with a familiar sense of peace as he looked out over the small patch of garden filled with verdant plants, desert wild-flowers, and a tumbling waterfall that always served as balm to his troubles. 'There is an underground spring that winds its way naturally to the surface and supplies the plants.'

'It's so gloriously untamed,' she said, her eyes glowing gold as she turned to him, genuine joy on her face. 'Don't get me wrong, the gardens at your residence are spectacular, but there's something about this place that's special.'

His heart clenched, and in that instant he knew.

This wasn't just about being captivated by a woman or her power to hold him enthralled.

This was the proverbial bolt of lightning his mother had always predicted, the kind of once-in-a-lifetime jolt experienced with a soulmate.

'Is there something wrong?'

She laid a tentative hand on his arm and he burned beneath her touch, wanting her hands all over his body, exploring, stroking, assuaging the need for her that threatened to consume him with its intensity.

He shook his head, using every ounce of self-control not to haul her into his arms and take her on the spot.

'I've never brought anyone here before. I was afraid you wouldn't understand.'

Her eyes widened, the tiny gold flecks glowing like the finest topaz as her hand left his arm to rise ever so slowly towards his face, where she gently cupped his cheek.

'I understand more than you think.'

Her other hand hovered near his chest before resting directly over his heart, and he knew she could feel how it pounded for her, how fast and furious the blood coursed through his veins with wanting her.

'Thank you for sharing this with me,' she murmured, standing on tiptoes to brush a soft kiss on his cheek.

With a primeval groan, he turned his head as

she pulled away, plastering his lips to hers while capturing both hands and anchoring them against his chest.

Like the few times they'd kissed before, she didn't hesitate, responding to him with eagerness and delight, firing his need for her with her honest reactions.

She set his blood alight, the intensity of his feelings making him want to do crazy things, like forget restraint and make her his as soon as possible.

But he couldn't. He had to think of Adhara, think of the future. Yet with her soft, pliant lips opening beneath his, almost begging him to enter her mouth and touch her tongue, he couldn't think at all.

Heat, blinding and intense, exploded through him as their tongues met, danced, dueled, and he knew that this fiery need between them so soon could jeopardise everything he'd worked so hard for.

However, he couldn't pull away.

He wanted more, he wanted all of her, to be his now and for ever.

All too soon she dragged her mouth away, as he drew in great, ragged breaths in the hope of quelling his desire.

It didn't work.

Nothing would, with the object of his desire staring at him with passion-hazed eyes gleaming like warm treacle, her frown at odds with the faint smile playing about the lips which begged him to return to exploring them.

'I—'

'It is all right,' he said, placing a fingertip against her lips. 'You do not need to say anything. It was a spur-of-the-moment thing.'

She lowered her hand and gestured towards the garden.

'Let's blame it on this place. Not that I'm into auras or anything, but something about being here feels so… right. Special.'

He couldn't speak as a lump of uncharacteristic emotion lodged in his throat. How had she done that, hone in on exactly how he felt whenever he came here?

The Oasis always brought comfort to him. He'd come here after his parents' death, after taking over the prince role full time, and he'd come here after his grandfather's death, seeking solace and peace and space away from the constant demands, grief and guilt that had dogged him.

He'd always believed in solitude to deal with his problems, yet suddenly he was glad he'd brought Bria here. She was more intuitive than he'd given her credit for, and sharing the Oasis with her had brought them closer.

He could feel it pulsing in the humid air between them, a definite link, an emotional pull, no matter how much she wanted to deny it.

'Can I ask you something?'

He nodded, knowing his ongoing silence must

seem strange to her, but not willing to speak while too many thoughts swirled through his head. Too many raw feelings were fighting their way to the surface of his recently exposed heart.

'Your marriage proposal was very cut and dried. Quite clearly focussed on business.'

She paused as if struggling for words, and he waited, curious as to where she was leading in her usual blunt fashion. 'Yet you also said you're interested in more.'

Her hand waved between them and she dropped it with an exasperated snort. 'What I'm trying to say is our attraction seems to be growing.'

'I'm glad to hear you admit it,' he murmured, tilting her chin up and searching her face for some clue as to how she felt. 'It is important for us both to be aware of how things will be between us as our relationship develops…'

He'd almost said 'when we marry', but he wasn't a born diplomat for nothing. Though she'd just admitted to their burgeoning attraction, he could see the haunted look in her eyes, the look of a woman who would flee at the slightest shift in dynamics.

'Developing relationship?'

She stiffened as his thumb stroked along her jawline, and he dropped his hand before he scared her away completely. Acknowledging the sizzle between them and acting on it were poles apart, considering she'd gone from sexy siren kissing him senseless one minute to wary and withdrawn the next.

'Relax, *gummur*. This does not complicate matters.'

She turned away and braced against the window frame, staring blindly out at the garden, but not before he'd glimpsed a flicker of fear in her hazel eyes.

'The way I see it, there is nothing to complicate. I'm here to do a job for a client, nothing more.'

'Is that what you call what exists between us? Nothing?'

The pulse in her neck picked up speed, telling him more than her forced casual words ever could.

'Yes.'

'Liar,' he whispered, sliding his hand into hers and gently tugging her towards him, exalted when she raised her eyes to his, the gold flecks in her eyes sparking with awareness. 'But do not worry. I am a patient man.'

'You think a few kisses will make me lose my mind and marry you?'

She tossed her hair back in defiance and he smiled, intertwining his fingers with hers, more than a little surprised when she didn't pull away.

'I think you will make the right decision, once you take the time to ponder my proposal with the logical business brain you possess. As for this—' he stroked her palm with his thumb once, twice, enjoying the flare of excitement in her eyes, the slight parting of her lips '—do not fight it. It is our destiny.'

He expected her to push him away.

He expected her to deny the palpable passion between them.

Instead, she slowly slid her hand from his and placed it against his heart; the pounding matched the pulse clearly visible in the soft hollow above her collarbone. The same soft hollow he'd spent many nights dreaming of kissing, of nibbling…

'There is nothing *logical* to any of this,' she murmured, her hand lingering a second longer before she let it drop and walked out the door.

Bria took several deep breaths as she strode into the garden, wishing she had the guts to take the car and leave His Highness alone in the desert.

The logical side of her brain was urging her to do it—the side which had suffered temporary amnesia for the last fifteen minutes, the side which had completely shut down since she'd set foot in this paradise.

She glanced around, the lush green foliage and staggering array of bright wild-flowers dazzling against the relentless sun, while the overpowering scent of orange blossom hung in the air, making her feel slightly lightheaded.

Though that probably had more to do with her loaded exchange with Sam than the amazing beauty of this place.

Why had she let down her guard?

Why here? Why now? Why him?

Shading her eyes, she glanced over her shoulder, half expecting him to come barging out of the house and take charge like he usually did. However, he was nowhere in sight, and she breathed a temporary sigh of relief, needing a few minutes to compose herself. She wouldn't give him the satisfaction of seeing how rattled she was by what had just happened.

What *had* just happened?

Slapping her sun hat onto her head for the limited protection it offered from the scorching sun, she veered away from the garden and back to the stone wall surrounding the compound in search of whatever limited shade she could get.

Her mind might be befuddled by the Prince, but she wasn't stupid enough to invite heat-stroke no matter how mad she was with herself.

Bracing herself against the wall, she closed her eyes, replaying the scene in the house through her mind like a movie on slow motion.

They'd connected.

They'd kissed.

They'd combusted.

She'd tried to pull away, tried to act like he'd cast some sadistic spell over her, tried to freeze him out with a half-hearted lie.

It hadn't worked.

He'd obviously seen the fire in her eyes, the simmering need, the banked heat whenever he came within two feet of her.

She could deny it all she liked, but what was developing between them had everything to do with emotion and little to do with logic.

And it terrified her.

Her head had always ruled her heart. It was the only way. But bit by bit Sam was chipping away at the protective barrier around her heart, and the more time she spent with him the more her fears escalated.

She didn't do emotion.

She never had, not when it came to men.

Especially *powerful* men, who expected her to bend to their will.

As for her decision, it was a no-brainer.

She couldn't contemplate marrying the Prince for one minute.

It was absurd. Daft. Totally and utterly insane.

Then why the imperceptible twang of pain deep down at the thought of walking away from him when her work here was done?

'You better come inside. The heat can be fe-
rocious.'

She raised her gaze to meet Sam's, wondering if he could read the torture in hers, the ridiculous indecision where her ever-reliable
logic warred with uncharacteristic emotion.

'You know this thing between us can never
develop into anything more.'

There, she'd said it, had vocalised what she'd
been thinking for a while now. Sadly, it
sounded as unconvincing as her lame self-talk.

A slow grin spread across his face, the confident grin of a man used to getting his own
way, of a man who wouldn't take no for an
answer.

'This thing? You will have to elaborate.'

'Don't be so obtuse,' she said, folding her
arms and doing her best not to pout. 'You seem
to have taken a few kisses out of context. As
for our attraction, it's nothing but a chemical
reaction. Happens all the time.'

His smile faded as quickly as it had come.

'You are attracted to other men all the time?'

'Of course not,' she snapped, realising her mistake the instant she spoke, as the corners of his mouth twitched with barely concealed amusement. 'What I meant was that people are attracted to each other all the time, but it doesn't mean they act on it. It's a part of life. Deal with it.'

'Oh, but I am dealing with it,' he said, his husky tone doing little to soothe her frazzled nerves as he stepped closer, shading her with a comforting cool much more effective than the wall at her back. 'You spoke of logic earlier. Surely you can see the logical way to deal with our attraction is to acknowledge it, nurture it, see what can come of it?'

'That's not logic, that's madness,' she muttered, her breath hitching as he braced his hands against the wall, effectively pinning her within the circle of his arms.

'You think this is madness?'

He lowered his head and nuzzled the soft spot behind her ear, his warm breath setting her skin alight as sensation ricocheted through her body, making a mockery of every 'logic' thought she'd ever entertained when it came to this man.

'Or perhaps this is madness?'

His lips trailed a row of tiny kisses along her neck, ending just above her collarbone, and she closed her eyes, knowing it was useless to fight something that felt this good, this right.

'Or maybe this?'

He brushed her mouth with his, a soft, feathery kiss like the fluttering of butterfly wings resting on a flower for a scant second, before taking flight again.

'Sam, please…'

As her pulse raced, her heart pounded and her body flamed with heat from his touch, rather than the scorching sun, she had no idea if she was pleading with him to stop or continue the pleasurable assault on her senses.

'As you wish, *gummur*. Come, lunch is served.'

He dropped his arms and stepped away, giving her all the space she needed to move. Now, if she could only get her wobbly knees to function…

'You have that effect on me too,' he murmured, offering her his hand while staring into her eyes with unabashed desire.

Sighing, she pushed off the wall, ignored his outstretched hand, and headed for the house.

She might have her pride, she might want to throttle him for turning her life upside down, and she might want to run as far from this infuriating, irresistible prince as possible—but a girl had to eat some time.

Bria sat back and patted her stomach.

'That was delicious.'

'Glad you enjoyed it.'

Sam started to clear away their dishes, and she stopped him. 'Let me. It's the least I can do after such a feast.'

He smiled. 'Zizi prepared the feast, all I did was dish it up. Besides, I never get to do the cleaning up. Indulge me.'

Damn, when he smiled like that, with every ounce of charm and persuasion in one power-packed glimpse of teeth beneath curving lips, she could indulge him in anything.

'Go ahead,' she said, waving him away, enjoying the sight of His Lordship doing a menial task like clearing the table.

She would've helped him if the spicy goat-kebabs wrapped in flat bread, almond *halwa* dripping in honey and fresh figs weren't sitting like a lump of lead in her stomach.

She shouldn't have eaten so much, but it had been easier to shovel food in her mouth and chew than make small talk after their earlier 'discussion'.

Thankfully, the meal had passed uneventfully, and as much as she liked the solitude of this place she couldn't wait to get back to the residence where there were other people around. Other people, to distract her from a powerful prince with piercing dark eyes who made her melt with a single glance.

'We should head back soon,' he said, staring at her from the doorway to the simple kitchen, his expression inscrutable. 'Unless you want to see more of the desert?'

'No, that's fine. I'm ready when you are.'

'Good.'

He strolled around the room, securing shutters, packing the wicker basket as if he was reluctant to leave, and she stifled a sigh, confused by her own hesitation at leaving this magical place.

He slipped into his suit jacket, the many medals jingling softly as he buttoned it. The formal white uniform should've looked incongruous in this heat, in these surroundings, but it merely added to his appeal. It gave him a regal air, adding to the powerful persona of the man.

'You are staring at my uniform. Is there a problem?'

Her gaze snapped up to his and she blushed, mortified he'd caught her staring.

'No, I was admiring it. It gives you an edge.'

He raised an eyebrow, a confident gleam making his eyes sparkle. 'You find my formal appearance appealing?'

Great, now she'd have to agree with him and sound like a simpering fool, or disagree and offend him.

'It suits you,' she said, simply settling for the truth.

Or downplaying it, considering she'd never seen a guy in uniform look so good. The crisp white enhanced his olive skin, the immaculate fit outlining his body to perfection.

'Thank you. The uniform is a part of who I

am, a part of my role as ruler when I'm here in Adhara.'

He paused, as if caught in some distant memory, before his lips curved upwards in a self-deprecating smile. 'Even though I miss the cut of my favourite Saville Row suits at times.'

She laughed. 'Well, I guess you can always take a flying visit to London.'

'Are you trying to get rid of me?'

His voice dropped to a low, husky murmur, the type of tone that chipped away at her defences, causing tiny cracks to appear in her well-constructed logic.

'Is it working?'

She deliberately kept her tone light, hoping he didn't hear the slight quiver as he breached the distance between them.

'Actually, I need to meet with my investors over the weekend in Dubai, but apart from that I'm all yours.'

Bria's mouth went dry and her heart jumped like a jackhammer at the intense look in his eyes.

'I'm all yours'...

Heck, what chance did a girl have against a Prince Charming act like that?

She knew spending one-on-one time with Sam was bad news, and after the day they'd just shared she knew she'd have to do some serious back-pedalling to avoid a major catastrophe—like acknowledging she felt more for the suave prince than she cared to admit.

'Isn't it time we left?'

Her swift change of topic didn't dampen the desire in his eyes, nor did it stop a knowing grin spreading across his face, so she snatched up the car keys and headed towards the door.

'If that is what you want,' he said, picking up the picnic basket and following her, pausing long enough to lock the front door before joining her at the car and holding his hand out for the keys.

'It is,' she muttered, knowing he must think she blew hotter and colder than the Adharan winds, as scorching days plunged into icy nights.

However, she'd lied.

Right now, she had no idea what she wanted, and the longer she spent in this country with this man the more confused she became.

Nothing was as clear cut as she needed it to be, and the uncertainty, the confusion she felt whenever she was with Sam, was worse than floundering in quicksand.

'I hope you enjoyed your day in the desert?'

Ignoring her inner turmoil, Bria fixed a polite smile on her face.

'It was memorable. Thanks for bringing me out here.'

'My pleasure. I hope it gave you another insight into this fascinating country.'

Bria nodded, captured by his potent stare, before turning away to look out of the side window.

Oh, she'd gained insight today.

However, she hadn't learned half as much about Adhara as she had about herself.

She wasn't as immune to Sam or as emotionally detached as she'd like to think.

And the realisation scared her beyond belief.

CHAPTER ELEVEN

BRIA stared at the computer screen, seeing but not quite believing the email resting like a dozing cobra in her in-box.

As if her day in the desert with Sam yesterday hadn't shredded her nerves already, she now had to face this.

Closing her eyes, she rubbed them gently, hoping to clear the incriminating words burned into her retinas. However, they were still there when she opened them, clear as day, a harsh reminder that, no matter how hard she fought her father, he had far-reaching tentacles like a nasty octopus.

The last year had been a sham.

Every client Motive had taken on, every design she'd done, had been tainted by the hand of Kurt Green.

He'd laid it all out for her in black and white in a 'catch up' email, hoping she didn't mind him sending all those clients her way but he had 'just wanted to help'.

Damn it, she'd been so careful in her screening, so sure the clients she had taken on had nothing to do with her father, yet here was the proof: names of holding companies he owned, companies who backed each and every one of her clients, including Ned Wilson.

She'd been so determined to succeed, to make a name for herself as the best in the business, without using the Green name.

And she'd done it—or so she'd thought.

Now, being the best architect in Australia meant nothing, considering who had manipulated her career, and the thought burned like boiling acid in her gut.

Picking up the nearest cushion, she placed it over her mouth and screamed in frustration, letting out her pent-up rage at being duped by the man she despised.

'Excuse me for intruding. Is everything all right?'

Bria cringed with embarrassment as Sam stuck his head around the door, with concern creasing his brow.

Sighing, she lowered the cushion. 'You heard that?'

He nodded. 'May I come in?'

'It's your palace,' she said, not in the mood for company, least of all the company of another man who had the capacity to tie her up in knots.

Striding across the room, he sat beside her, and she instantly wished she could pick up the cushion again, though this time to hug it to her chest for a bit of useless protection against his imposing presence.

'You did not answer my question. Is everything all right?'

'Not really.'

Bria forced her fingers to still when she realised she was plucking at the cushion tassels, fraying the ends as badly as her nerves.

'What is wrong? Is there anything I can do to help?'

'Not unless Adharan laws extend to beheading.'

Sam frowned, and she could've laughed out loud at his confusion if her red-hot anger had subsided long enough.

'You'll have to excuse my black humour. I've just had an email from my father.'

'And you would like his head to be chopped off?'

As Sam's eyebrows shot up, Bria managed a wry chuckle. 'Believe me, beheading would be too good for him.'

'I do not understand.'

'Neither do I,' she muttered, wishing Sam would leave her to manage her bitterness in peace, while a small part of her was grateful he appeared to care.

'Look, it's just my father up to his old tricks, trying to control me. Interfering in my life, meddling in my business. He's impossible.'

Sam shook his head and reached towards her, pity in his eyes, and this time she grabbed the cushion and held it close.

Having him listen to her was one thing—having him touch her when she could quite easily fall apart any second was another.

Everything about this man screamed he was nothing like her father, despite her preconceived ideas. Yet there had been several indications that Sam had done the same, manipulating circumstances to suit him.

Could she really trust him? Could a man who had so much power, more so than her father, be any different?

Could he actually have a heart?

'I am sorry for your troubles.'

Sam shrugged and let his hand drop to his lap, something akin to hurt flickering in his eyes at her obvious rebuff. 'If there is anything I can do, please let me know.'

'Thanks,' she said, feeling like a cold-hearted cow, but too distraught, too disillusioned, to care as her gaze flicked to the computer screen like a moth drawn to a particularly foul flame.

Everything she'd strived for, everything she'd built, was a sham. Her business was her life, but if she couldn't establish a name for herself without her father's malevolent strings-attached help, what could she do?

Suddenly, a blinding flash of clarity sent her blood pressure skyrocketing as she shut her eyes against the monstrous thought.

There was one way to ensure her reputation as a top architect, one way to erase the nightmare of being manipulated by a man she'd spent a lifetime trying to escape.

However, it involved compromising her principles, and going against every independent instinct that told her to make a run for it while she still could.

Agreeing to marry Sam was the last thing she wanted to do.

But what if it could give her the one thing she wanted the most?

'Bria? I am worried about you.'

This time she didn't flinch as he reached out and cupped her cheek. Instead, she savoured his gentle touch for a long, exquisite moment, before opening her eyes, unprepared for the depth of caring in his.

'I'll be fine,' she said, a lump of emotion lodging in her throat as she placed her hand over his, trying to convey her gratitude with a simple touch.

They didn't move for what seemed like an

eternity, the heat from his palm branding her cheek, her fingers tempted to press his hand closer so he would never let go.

'If you're sure?'

Sure? She wasn't sure of anything, least of all how a woman who was never frivolous could take a chance on emotion. It had never happened before. And it wouldn't happen now. It just wasn't worth it in the long run.

But what if it was too late?

'I'm sure.'

She dropped her hand and broke the contact between them by turning her face away on the pretext of reaching for a glass of water. Anything to break the spellbinding tension which had her yearning to fling herself into his arms for whatever comfort he could give.

'In that case, I will leave you.'

Sam inclined his head, stood and strode to the door, his movements strangely formal after the intimacy they'd just shared.

'Sam?'

He stopped with his hand on the doorknob. 'Yes?'

'Thanks,' she said, sending him a tremulous smile, hating how her bottom lip wobbled at the warmth in his answering smile.

'You're welcome.'

She waited till the door closed before collapsing back onto the sofa, her earlier anger replaced by a much scarier emotion.

An emotion she dared not label for fear of acknowledging that she felt more for Sam than was good for her.

'I am leaving.'

Bria looked up from her work book and set it aside, the sight of Sam in full uniform taking her breath away.

'Business?'

He nodded and pulled up a garden chair beside her. 'Meetings with my investors have been brought forward. I'm off to Dubai shortly, and won't be back till Sunday.'

'Uh-huh.'

She tried to sound casual, as if Sunday didn't mean a thing to her, when in fact they both knew that was the day he expected an answer to his proposal.

An answer which had been cut and dried until that damn email.

'If there is anything you need while I am away ask Rasha. She will organise whatever you need.'

'Thanks.'

Folding her hands in her lap, she waited. Sam's tone may sound perfunctory and businesslike, but there was something more behind this farewell. She could see it in the glow of his dark eyes, the intense expression on his face.

'Before I go, I would like to give you something.'

He withdrew a small black-velvet box from

the breast pocket of his jacket, took hold of her hand and gently pressed it into her palm before wrapping her fingers around it.

Startled, she stared at the box as if it was a scorpion with a particularly nasty sting in its tail.

'Consider this a gift. A token of appreciation for considering my proposal.'

She shook her head, her gaze drawn to the box repeatedly.

'I can't accept it.'

'You do not know what it is yet,' he said, his amusement audible as he tapped the lid of the box. 'Go on, open it. I insist.'

'Well, if you insist.'

Her sarcasm was lost on him as his satisfied smile grew, her fingers turning the box over and over rather than opening it.

'Let me,' he said, stilling her hand and flipping open the box in a deft movement.

Bria held her breath as he turned the box

towards her, and she slowly exhaled on a soft 'Wow,' as she unconsciously reached out to caress the beautiful opal pendant nestled there.

'You like it?'

The uncertainty in his voice tugged at her heart, and she looked up, unprepared for the depth of feeling in his eyes.

'It's incredible,' she said, her gaze drawn to the fiery stone again, its rich sapphire-and-emerald facets flashing in the sunlight.

Lifting the opal from its resting place, he leaned towards her.

'I know how much your ring means to you, and I thought it would be nice to have something to go with it. Something that hopefully will also come to mean more to you.'

Her breath caught as his fingers brushed the nape of her neck, sensation skittering through her body as he fastened the clasp and the opal came to rest between her breasts.

'Exquisite,' he said, his finger tracing the

white-gold necklace along her neckline, and stopping just short of the pendant.

Bria's head swam, whether from the heat of the day, the heady orange-blossom scent pervading the lush garden, Sam's proximity, or his hope that this gift would come to mean more to her.

'I—I don't know what to say,' she said, hypnotised by his stare, captured by his hand which had drifted to her shoulder and drew her inexorably towards him.

'You do not have to say anything.'

His lips brushed hers in a soft, lingering kiss before he pulled away, regret etched across the powerful planes of his face.

'This is my gift to you. Regardless of what happens between us in the future, I want you to have it.'

She should've refused it, as had been her first intention.

She should've pushed him for answers to what was really going on between them.

Instead, she placed her hand over the pendant, and felt it grow hot beneath her palm like a mood-stone centred on the man who had given it to her.

'Thank you,' she said, blinking back sudden tears at the generosity of his gift and what it might mean for them.

'My pleasure, *gummur*.'

Reaching out, he cupped her cheek for one long, loaded moment before standing abruptly and moving away. 'Until Sunday.'

'Until Sunday,' she echoed softly, watching the man she'd developed feelings for stroll through the garden till he disappeared from sight.

Suddenly, she sat bolt upright.

The man she'd developed feelings for?

Oh, no…

Oh, yes!

Somewhere between Melbourne and Adhara, between strolling through the Werribee

Mansion gardens and sharing a simple lunch at the Oasis, she had allowed him to breach her defences and make her *feel*.

Despite every self-preservation mechanism telling her otherwise, despite her strong principles telling her she could never live with a power-driven man like a prince, she'd gone ahead and done it anyway.

She'd fallen for a man totally wrong for her.

A prince, a ruler, a businessman who needed her architectural expertise yet wanted more.

The opal glowed hot in her fingers as she pondered Sam's power over her, which instantly evoked thoughts of her father. Both men ruled their own worlds and had people only too eager to do their bidding. Both were used to controlling situations and circumstances.

Was that where the similarities ended? Her father was a control freak and a born manipulator—was Sam any different?

Was the Prince, who could have any woman

in the world, trying to control this situation—
and her—by manipulating her into a marriage
for reasons only known to him?

If so, why would he have given her a gift he
knew would mean more to her than any priceless jewellery he could afford?

Why would he have spent the last few days
courting her, wooing her, showing her glimpses
of his inner self, if there wasn't something
more to his proposal?

Fear streaked through her body as a tiny
blossom of an emotion she dared not define
unfurled within her heart at the thought he
might have feelings for her.

After all, actions spoke louder than words,
and he'd just given her a pretty good indication
she meant more to him than an adjunct to fur-
thering his country's development.

Her head ached with unanswered questions
and supposition, and, hot on the heels of her startling realisation that she had fallen for him, it

made her feel like she'd been out in the sun too long.

At least she'd have a reprieve from his powerful presence over the next few days.

But what then?

And why did the thought that she wouldn't see him for three days leave her sadder than she could've anticipated?

Twirling the opal between her fingers, she headed for the welcoming cool of the house and the peaceful serenity of her room.

She needed time to think.

She needed time to absorb the startling fact she'd fallen for a prince who might have the same characteristics she loathed in her father.

CHAPTER TWELVE

'So, how was the trip? You look fabulous, and I'm guessing seeing Yusif has something to do with that?'

Lou laughed and shrugged out of Bria's embrace, plopping onto the nearest sofa.

'He's fine. Busy, but we managed to spend every spare minute together.'

A faint pink stained her friend's tanned cheeks, and Bria held up her hand. 'Please, by the looks of that blush, I don't want to hear any details of how you spent those spare minutes.'

'I miss him so much, Bree.'

A shadow passed over Lou's normally bright face as Bria wondered what it would be like to love someone like that: so thoroughly, so completely.

Usually, she wouldn't have cared, but since admitting she had feelings for Sam a small part of her wanted to find out.

'I know you do.'

She squeezed Lou's hand as she took a seat next to her. 'I've got something that might keep you occupied while you wait for him to come back.'

'Sounds intriguing!' Lou sat up, her eyes sparkling. 'Do tell.'

Bria laughed and reached for the sketch-pad propped next to the computer.

'I haven't formalised anything yet, but I've spent some time checking out mosaics, getting a feel for what's around, and I've made some preliminary sketches for this client's house. Just a few rough ideas, mind you, but I thought you could give me some feedback?'

'Sure,' Lou said, taking the pad and flicking through the pages. 'After all, I'm an authentic

Adharan now, and this guy wants an authentic Adharan house, right?'

Bria nodded and held her breath. Similar to when a client looked at her work for the first time, her stomach knotted with nerves as Lou flipped page after page.

'Well, what do you think?'

Lou finally looked up, her eyes wide and filled with admiration.

'Bree, it's incredible. Gorgeous! This client of yours is one lucky guy.'

Bria laughed, hoping Ned Wilson would be half as thrilled as her friend.

'Great, well, I guess my work here is nearly done. Once I finalise details to get the mosaics shipped to Sydney, it's all systems go.'

In more ways than one.

Her research trip here would be done, and Sam would get his final answer.

Lou sat back and held her at arm's length. 'I know you said you'd only be here to check out ideas for this Ned guy, but do you really have to go?'

Bria nodded, not trusting herself to speak, considering tears clogged her throat.

'So the Prince hasn't swept you off your feet?'

Bria swallowed a lump the size of a rock in her throat, hating the white lie she had to tell her friend. 'Afraid not.'

Her hand drifted to her neck, where she fiddled with the opal pendant—something she'd found herself doing on an increasingly frequent basis since Sam had given it to her.

'Wow, that's some rock around your neck.' Lou bent to take a closer look, wolf-whistling under her breath. 'It's stunning.'

'It is, isn't it?'

Bria turned away and fiddled with the growing pile of quotes from the various vendors she'd contacted for the mosaics, wishing she could blurt the whole truth out to her friend, but knowing she needed more time to assimilate it herself before articulating her crazy dreams out loud.

'Did you pick it up while I was away?'

'Uh-huh.'

Hoping she wouldn't go to hell for two little white lies in under thirty seconds, she quickly changed the subject.

'When's Yusif due back?'

Lou rolled her eyes. 'When Samman gets his butt into gear and finishes schmoozing some investors.'

Bria bit back a smile. Personally, she hoped Sam would get his butt back here pronto, so she could inform him of her momentous decision, the decision that would change both their lives for ever.

Lou propped against the desk and rifled through the top sketches, a thoughtful expression on her face.

'You know, this guy's place is going to be something else. Maybe you should stick around so I can commission you to design something for Yusif and me.'

'You never know your luck,' Bria said, making light of her comment with a hearty laugh when Lou turned startled, wide eyes to her. 'Now, I need to do some more work here, so if you don't mind? Ned is a bit of a slave driver, and wants his house done ASAP.'

Lou chuckled and held up her hands. 'Okay, okay, I get the hint. I'll see you later.'

Bria's practised smile stayed firmly in place till Lou shut the door, then she collapsed back onto the sofa.

Phew, that had been close.

She knew she could trust Lou, could tell her anything, but right now she could hardly comprehend what she was contemplating let alone articulate it out loud.

Could she really stay in Adhara—create a new capital city? Become Sam's wife? Become *royalty*?

Such outrageous thoughts, yet since her emotional barriers had crumbled she had no option but to acknowledge what was in her heart.

Sighing, she sat back and closed her eyes, wriggling when something hard dug into her back.

Turning around, she pulled the book Sam had given her during the tour of the palace from behind a cushion and smiled, caressing the worn leather on the cover. She hadn't had a chance to read any of it, given most of her time had been spent in Sam's company.

Curious, she flipped several pages, speed-reading through the history of this tiny country. She'd grown to like its many contrasts—the eclectic mix of French, English and Arabic cultures mixing to form an interesting blend. The people here were proud of their heritage and lived in peace, and in a way she could see Sam was a part of that.

He ruled with a velvet glove, soft yet firm, putting the needs of his country first while trying to maintain a modern outlook. It couldn't be easy, having that responsibility all the time, having your every move watched and criticized, but he took it in his stride. His casual approach to life was a surprise, considering his sovereignty.

He really was a special man. Luckily for her, she'd finally figured it out.

Suddenly, her gaze focussed on the start of the second chapter—or, more precisely, the rules of accession.

The only way an Adharan prince can ascend to the throne and be crowned king is by marrying.

Doubt pierced Bria's internal bubble of happiness, and it popped with a resounding, painful bang.

Was this the missing piece of the puzzle? The 'something more' she'd felt Sam had kept from her about his proposal right from the beginning?

Bria flicked through the next few pages frantically, searching for answers to the questions buzzing through her brain, before she recognised her quest as useless and snapped the book shut.

Sam had never married.

He had a reputation as a playboy.

So why the sudden need for a wife now? Why the need to be king now?

Bria's fingers twisted the chiffon scarf draped around her neck into knots as an answer she didn't want to contemplate flashed into her mind.

Sam wanted Adhara City rebuilt.

He wanted it to rival other mega cities.

He wanted his country thrust into the twenty-first century in a big way.

And he wanted her to do it.

But what if other people weren't so impressed by his modern outlook, by his lifestyle?

What if the investors he seemed hell bent on

impressing would be more convinced by a king rather than a playboy prince?

The pieces of the puzzle slid into place as Bria's heart froze, fractured and splintered into a thousand icy fragments.

She'd thought Sam's kisses had meant something.

She'd thought the way he'd opened up to her had indicated a depth of feeling she'd never believed in until now.

She'd thought the opal meant he cared.

She'd thought wrong on all counts.

Lord, what a fool she'd been. Men like Sam didn't fall for women like her. They were different on so many levels: culturally, socially and emotionally, the latter most of all.

After all, she could handle the other differences—it was the fact he didn't feel a thing for her beyond a means to an end, while she'd let him breach her defences and had been foolish enough to let him near her heart.

It all made sense now.

His quick-fire interest in her.

His absurd proposal and the speed with which he expected an answer.

His pretending to care.

Oh, yes, perfect sense, and she had better things to do with her time than stick around here and be played for a fool, starting with booking the first available flight out of the country.

But not before she'd given the Prince a piece of her mind.

Samman stared at the figures before his eyes till they swam. Not that he needed to. He'd studied the projections for the new Adhara City for the last few months, had built in leeway for every contingency, had planned to the nth degree.

Now all he needed was for the final investors to sign on the dotted line, and he would have fulfilled his dream for his country and kept his promise to his grandfather.

It was almost done but for one important factor: his marriage to Bria.

He needed her.

Needed her to marry him for the crown to be his, needed her expertise, needed her by his side to impress the investors who still didn't trust him despite his reassurances—needed her full-stop.

The last thought startled him, and he pushed away from his desk and strode to the window of his thirtieth-floor penthouse, staring out at the glittering lights of Dubai.

He loved this city, had seen it develop with the speed of light, and while he knew Adhara City wouldn't be on the same scale he wanted the same expansion for his country.

New shopping malls, new hotels, new resorts would all mean a tourism boom and a thriving economy for his people. Jobs, commerce, development; it was all within reach if only he could get these final investors on board.

It was his dream, had been a part of his grand-father's dream, but right now all he could focus on were dreams of another kind.

Dreams haunted by a beautiful woman dressed in the soft silk of his country, a woman with hair the colour of his desert, and eyes like warm honey.

He'd intended the opal to be a betrothal gift, for he had no doubt she would agree to his proposal, considering the business aspect of it. But when he'd been called away suddenly he hadn't been able to wait, struck by a strange impulse to give it to her in remembrance of him.

Even now, the thought of the fiery stone nestled between her breasts sent a surge of such intense longing through him, he gripped the window sill for support.

A sharp knock distracted him from his thoughts, and he turned to find Hakim staring at him with a curious expression.

'What is it?'

Hakim held out the cordless phone to him. 'It is Rasha. She says it's urgent.'

Samman raised an eyebrow, surprised his PA had bothered him with this. Hakim handled emergencies for him on a daily basis, and he really wasn't in the mood to deal with an over-emotional maid right now.

'Take care of it.'

Hakim almost squirmed, his discomfort obvious. 'She said it is about Miss Green.'

Samman froze, a thousand horrible scenarios flashing through his head as he reached for the phone as if in slow motion.

He calmed somewhat as he listened to Rasha's frantic tones, thankful his Bria hadn't been maimed or wounded, or worse.

However, he froze at her final words and, as he barked instructions at her, his mind was already focussed on what he had to do for the next few hours, well aware of the impact it would have on his life.

After hanging up, he thrust the phone into a bewildered Hakim's hand.

'Cancel my meetings for today. I must leave immediately.'

'But Your Highness—'

'Just do it.'

Samman lowered his voice with effort, his mind already elsewhere, but unable to ignore the fact his PA had just uttered a protest directed at him when he'd never questioned an order before.

'Is there a problem, Hakim?'

Hakim cleared his throat, turning the phone over and over in his hands.

'It is not my place to question you, Your Highness. I have worked for you for many years, my father worked for your grandfather for many years, and it is this association that prompts me to speak up.'

'Get to the point.'

'Yes, sir.'

Hakim bowed his head as if ashamed to look

at him. 'If I may be so bold to say, this Miss Green has you chasing your tail like a mountain goat. First in Melbourne, now in Adhara—you are not yourself, and it troubles me. There has been talk you would enter into an arranged marriage when we returned from Australia, and then you met her. I know your dreams for our country. I know your grandfather's dreams, and I am worried…'

Hakim trailed off and Samman stared at him in shock, anger rooting him to the spot at the insubordination shown to him by a cherished member of his staff.

However, his anger faded as quickly as it had come. He trusted Hakim as his grandfather had trusted Hakim's father, and if he'd been bold enough to risk his job by speaking out like this he must be truly concerned.

Besides, Hakim was right. Bria did have him running around in circles, and what he had to do over the next few hours proved it.

'Do not worry, Hakim. Everything will work out, you will see.'

Hakim slowly raised his head, his eyes filled with hope rather than the dread Samman had glimpsed a few moments ago.

'And, though I should send you into exile for speaking to me like that, I forgive you in the interests of our familial links.'

'Thank you, Your Highness.'

Hakim bowed and made a hasty retreat, while Samman picked up his mobile phone and wallet and headed for the door.

He wouldn't need anything else where he was going.

Apart from a persuasive manner, that was.

And a healthy dose of honesty.

Bria had nodded off, the drone of the car's engine lulling her into a half-doze which she welcomed. Anything was better than having recriminating thoughts reverberating around her head, like a squash ball rebounding off the walls of a court.

She couldn't have been stupid enough to want to marry a prince. It had had to be the lure of making a name for herself after her father's email.

Yeah, that had to be it. The ever-present desire to shrug off the shackles of her upbringing must've affected her brain.

Then why the persistent ache in the vicinity of her heart? And it did ache, with every breath she took, with every mile between her and the man she'd been stupid enough to fall for.

She should be thankful. She'd had a lucky escape, finding out the truth before it was too late. However, she didn't feel lucky. She felt downright rotten, and knew it would take her a lifetime to get over Sam.

'We're almost there.'

Bria's eyes fluttered open, her surroundings strangely disorientating. She might have been half-asleep for the last few hours, but there was no way they'd been travelling for the half day it would have taken them to get to Dubai.

'Rasha, this isn't downtown Dubai,' she said, filled with a sudden foreboding as she recognised several landmarks, including an imposing stone wall and the small abode behind it.

'No, it isn't.'

Rasha pulled up outside the front door, and Bria watched in wide-eyed horror as it slowly opened and out stepped the one man she'd hoped to give a final tongue-lashing to in the confines of his office.

She could've handled facing him in some cold, glass, professional interior to deliver a few home truths. Instead, she now had to face him in a place which held treasured memories for them both.

'The Prince is waiting,' Rasha said, her tone typically subservient, like everyone who worked for Sam.

'Let him wait,' Bria muttered, marshalling every ounce of indignation she'd felt when she'd first learned the truth about his coronation, trying to focus on fuelling her anger, rather than noticing how incredible Sam looked silhouetted against the sinking sun.

This was it, the end of the road.

Time to do what she should've done as soon as she'd set foot in this country: tell the Prince his fortune.

CHAPTER THIRTEEN

BRIA glared at Sam as he wrenched open the passenger door, apparently oblivious to her simmering temper.

'Thank you, Rasha. That will be all.'

'How could you?' Bria muttered in Rasha's direction, surprised to see the sheen of tears in the young woman's eyes.

'I am sorry. He is the Prince. It is my duty.'

Shaking her head, Bria fiddled with her seatbelt latch. Rasha might have done her duty, but there was no way she was getting out of this car in a hurry. Let His Highness stew.

'*Gummur*, I am a forceful man, and unless you want me to drag you from the car I strongly suggest you get out of your own accord.'

'I'm not "your love".'

She spat the words in his face, enjoying the shock dilating his pupils, the fleeting flicker of hurt.

'Our meeting was supposed to take place in Dubai. I have a plane to catch afterwards.'

He shrugged, a determined expression on his face. 'Don't say I didn't warn you.'

With surprising speed he reached across her, pinning her body to the seat with his own, assaulting her senses with the scent of sandalwood, the feel of his rock-hard chest and a palpable heat radiating off him in seductive waves.

She gasped, unprepared for the physical contact, and he turned his head slightly, bringing his lips within inches of her own.

'Perhaps it is not so unpleasant to have a man take charge.'

His husky whisper sent a shiver through her body, and it wasn't of revulsion.

She should've pushed him away, shoved him out the door and slammed it on his big head.

However, she might be heartbroken, but she wasn't entirely stupid. Rasha would do whatever Sam wanted, and unless she wanted to sit in the car till she melted there was no way she was going anywhere.

With a final glare in his direction, she unlatched her seatbelt with a decisive click, and Sam pulled back, giving her space to slide it off her shoulder.

'Now, do you think you can walk inside so we can talk, or would you prefer it if I carried you?'

Sending him a scathing glance, Bria slid from the car and marched towards the house, head held high.

This wouldn't take long.

In fact, telling the officious prince where he could stick his proposal wouldn't take long at all.

So much for this place being an oasis.

She'd thought it a welcoming haven the first time he'd brought her here, but not now. Stepping through the stone walls, she felt as though her world was closing in on itself, and there wasn't one damn thing she could do about it.

Turning in the doorway, she gaped as Sam carried her luggage towards her, while Rasha drove the car away as if she had a pack of demons on her tail.

'What do you think you're doing?'

She planted her hands on her hips, needing something to anchor them before she reached out and wrapped them around his neck and squeezed hard.

'You are not going to the airport.'

He dropped the luggage inside the door and slammed it shut. 'We need to talk.'

'Like I have any choice,' she said, sending him a venomous look which would've frozen a lesser man. Predictably, it had little effect on the stubborn prince.

'You have a choice,' he said, indicating that she should take a seat while he sat opposite. 'But only after you tell me what this ridiculous fleeing is all about.'

She ignored the seat, preferring to stand and take what little satisfaction she could get by towering over him.

'What I do, where I go and when, is no concern of yours.'

'That's where you're wrong.'

He leaped out of the chair and grabbed her arms before she had a chance to react, his body way too close to hers, invading her personal space in a way only he could.

'I am concerned about you.'

She laughed, a harsh, bitter sound that made the hackles on her neck stand to attention.

'Oh yes, I'm sure you are. After all, the welfare of your much-needed wife before you're crowned king must be paramount, this close to sealing the deal.'

He didn't flinch.

He didn't deny it.

Instead, he squared his shoulders as if marching into battle.

'I have already laid out the business aspect of my proposal. Why are you behaving like this?'

'Cut the crap,' she said, struggling to free herself, but only succeeding in getting more frustrated when Sam tightened his grip. 'You lied to me. Your *business proposal* centred on my architectural skills—not the fact you needed a wife ASAP to obtain a crown.'

Or the fact that any woman would probably do, something that hurt way more than it should.

This time she scored a direct hit, as a slight pink stained his tanned cheeks.

'I did not lie to you. I did not think it was relevant to discuss all facets of my coronation with you at such an early stage.'

Rage rendered her speechless, surging through her body like lava bubbling beneath the surface of a simmering volcano, before exploding forth in a fiery torrent she had no chance of stopping.

'Don't you get it?' she yelled at him, taking little pleasure from the startled look on his face. 'There would've been *no* stage where withholding information like that would've been acceptable. What was I supposed to do—pretend to have a clue what being a queen in this country would entail? Polish your crown for you? Act like a trophy wife?'

She planted her palms against his chest and pushed hard, needing to get away from him, needing to cool down before she did something totally out of character, like slap him.

He didn't budge.

'Want to know the hilarious bit? You picked the wrong woman in every respect. I'd never be some guy's trophy, I'd never be the meek and mild type to stand there and not speak my mind. So, guess what? Maybe I've done you a favour—saved you from losing your precious bloody investors once and for all.'

She pushed again, using every ounce of her strength, and he still didn't move an inch, his eyes sparking with interest rather than anger.

When he spoke the words were so soft she had to lean forward a fraction to hear him.

'I did not pick the wrong woman.'

Before she could register the intent behind his words, he crushed her lips beneath his in a demanding, mind-blowing kiss which left her more breathless and confused than ever.

Now was her chance to shove him away.

Instead, her fingers curled into the crisp cotton business-shirt, anchoring herself in a world gone mad.

Her mouth flowered beneath his like a desert blossom in the sun, desperate for heat, craving more. Sam didn't need a second invitation, his tongue exploring her mouth with thorough possessiveness, challenging her to match him.

Molten heat flowed through her body as she clung to him, rage transforming to lust in a second, her anger forgotten under the sensual assault of his lips, his hands.

He'd never touched her like this, skimming her body with long, slow caresses from shoulder to hip along the length of her back, making her arch into him, wanting more. Needing more.

As if sensing her secret desires, his lips left hers and trailed down her neck in soft, hot, open-mouthed kisses that had her melting into him with little resistance.

She couldn't stop this.

It was like trying to outrun a sandstorm: totally and utterly useless.

'*Habibati*,' he murmured, nuzzling the hollow above her collarbone, and she stiffened, wondering what he'd just called her, hating how such a simple word uttered in the throes of passion could accentuate the yawning differences between them.

'Sam, don't.'

Bria twisted her head, succeeding at last in shoving him away, before quickly dropping her hands when she realised they'd lingered a fraction too long on his chest.

'Don't what—kiss you? Want you?'

He shrugged, a patient expression on his face as if he had all the time in the world for her to come to her senses.

'It is useless to ask me to do such things. I cannot stop wanting you. I cannot stop hoping that you feel the same way, and will want to stay in my country as my wife.'

Bria shook her head, wondering what it would take to get through to this guy. He was so used to getting his own way in everything that he wouldn't take no for an answer. Maybe he was more like her father than she'd supposed, and the thought sent a shiver of dread through her.

'Wanting someone doesn't equate to feeling. Wanting someone isn't a foundation to build a marriage on. You of all people should know that.'

He stiffened as if she'd slapped him, and she stepped back a fraction, nervous she'd gone too far.

'What do you mean?'

Knowing this might be the only chance to alienate him, to drive home her point and get the hell out of this country, she said, 'You want something, you get it. That's what having power is all about. But wanting to possess things and wanting to possess a person are worlds apart. Wanting me to further your own agenda is tantamount to my being manipulated and controlled, and I've had a lifetime of what that feels like already.'

Sam paled as if she'd struck him, and her heart twisted with pain at what she was doing, what she had to do to save herself.

'You're saying I'm like your father?'

She'd expected a raging torrent of abuse.

She'd expected a flash of temper to rival her own earlier.

She never expected to see Sam deflate before her eyes, his shoulders sag, and his face age ten years as he nodded.

'You are right.'

With those three little words, he turned and walked out the door.

CHAPTER FOURTEEN

SAMMAN staggered into the garden, blinded by a sudden, overwhelming realisation.

He'd been so focussed on doing what was right for his country, doing what was right for him, that he'd ignored one salient fact.

Bria.

Her needs. Her wants.

Sinking onto a stone bench, he dropped his head in his hands, allowing the emptiness to fill him, to consume him, to dull the ache which spread like a cancerous growth, eating away at his soul till he had nothing left to give.

He'd never gotten over his guilt at the role he might've played in his grandfather's death: the constant rows, the constant battle of wills, the way he'd asserted his own needs and insisted on finding his own wife to the detriment of what the old man had wanted. The stress must've contributed to his heart attack, and Sam had never forgiven himself.

It was why he'd been so focussed on fulfilling his grandfather's dying wish for Adhara.

It was why he'd recently realised it was time to agree to an arranged marriage, despite his yearning for a wife to love.

However, it looked like he hadn't learned a thing.

He'd treated Bria the same way—putting his own needs first, pushing her to want him, to love him, forcing her to acknowledge something which might not even exist other than in his own head.

He was a fool.

And thanks to his selfishness he was about to lose the woman he loved.

'Sam, are you all right?'

He stiffened at her tentative touch on his shoulder, all too aware he would never be all right again once she walked out of his life.

'Please, look at me. I'm sorry. I should never have said what I did.'

He raised his head, the pain on her face mirroring his own.

'Why not? You spoke the truth.'

She sat next to him and covered his hand with hers, so soft and pale against his olive skin. 'I wanted to hurt you as much as you've hurt me. You're nothing like my father…'

She trailed off, her eyes scanning his face for—what? Forgiveness? An explanation?

Her grip tightened, the gentle pressure reassuring, and he found himself speaking without realising it.

'Yes, I am. He wants to control your life, I was trying to do the same. From the first minute I saw you I wanted you, and I did everything in my power to make that happen.'

'Wanted me for your wife, you mean?'

He dragged in a deep breath, hating what came next, but finding a strange comfort in divulging the whole truth to her.

What would it matter when she left him anyway?

'Yes, I wanted you for my wife. As you've already guessed, I need to be crowned king as soon as possible to gain the support of the investors. They do not trust me, believing my reputation to be a liability. To become king sooner rather than later was my only option to secure Adhara's future.'

Bria didn't move a muscle or look away. Instead, her eyes glowed with sadness, and he continued.

'I made a promise to my grandfather on his deathbed: I would do everything in my power to take Adhara into the future, to make it a country to be reckoned with. That time is now. I have wasted enough time searching...'

Silence stretched between them, broken by the soft gurgle of the underwater spring as it bubbled to the surface and splashed over rocks eroded by time and nature.

'Searching for what?'

Closing his eyes, he knew he'd have to tell her all of it.

'Searching for a woman I loved enough to become my wife.'

He heard Bria's soft gasp of shock, could imagine the expression of disbelief on her face.

'But I thought you'd already found her?'

He shook his head and opened his eyes, hoping she could read the sincerity there.

'No, I was being truthful when I said there had been no one special. You assumed I had loved someone.'

Bria frowned, confusion creasing her brow. 'But you said you and your grandfather fought over a suitable bride.'

'Yes, we fought all the time. He wanted me

to marry for my country, I wanted to marry for love, just like my parents.'

Bria's frown deepened as she shook her head. 'Then why me? Or were you so desperate to catapult Adhara into the developmental stratosphere you'd settle for anyone?'

'You do not know?'

Sam sighed, wishing he could haul her into his arms and show her what was in his heart, rather than try to explain a love this powerful, this deep.

He reached for her hand, holding on tightly when she struggled as if to withdraw it.

'Yes, I admit my first thoughts were for my country, but from the minute I saw you I knew you were the woman for me. I knew you were the one.'

Bria's mouth dropped open as she struggled to comprehend the words coming out of Sam's mouth.

'What are you saying?'

He reached up and cupped her cheek, the

tenderness in his dark eyes taking her breath away.

'I'm saying that my mother was right. She always said love was like being hit by a lightning bolt, and that's exactly how I felt when I first saw you: shocked, connected, electrified. And those feelings only intensified the longer we spent together. I wanted to give you time to adjust, time to make the right decision, in the hope you would feel the same for me. I wanted you to be my wife for real. To realise that I love you. That I want you by my side for ever.'

For a brief moment, an indescribable joy burst like a shooting star rocketing through her body.

Until reality set in and she realised that a proud man like Sam, a powerful man who put his country before everything, would say anything to get what he wanted—including profess a love for her in the hope she'd marry him to secure his precious investors.

'I can't,' she murmured, staring at her hands

clenched firmly in her lap, wishing that half of what he'd said was real.

To have his love, to live the rest of her life with him, would be a dream come true. But stuff like that didn't happen, at least not to her.

'You do not love me.'

His flat monotone would've broken her heart if he hadn't already achieved that when he'd confirmed the need to be betrothed to be king, all in the name of his country.

'Bria? Look at me.'

She shook her head, her gaze fixed on her fingers which plucked at her cotton skirt, leaving a trail of tiny wrinkles. However, she couldn't avoid looking at him for ever, and when he placed a fingertip under her chin and tilted it up she had no option but to meet his grave gaze.

His eyes skimmed her face, searching, probing, as if seeking the answers to all his questions. 'Tell me what is in your heart.'

Bria glanced away, knowing the truth would only serve to prolong the agony between them, but unable to lie with his open, direct gaze on her.

'Tell me!'

She jumped, startled by the command in his voice, and suddenly there was no question about lying.

So what if she had feelings?

It didn't change a thing. He'd probably still made up that whole 'I love you' bit to get her onside, and there was no way she'd fall for it.

Wrenching away from him, she said, 'Fine. You want to hear it? Of course I have feelings. Against my better judgement, I let you slip under my guard. You intrigued me from the very beginning, and I even might've called you, when lo and behold you turn out to be some fancy-schmancy prince rather than the man I thought you were. I should've kept my distance then, but no. I spend time with you, I kiss you, I grow to love you, and then this.'

She blew out an exasperated breath, tired of the emotions churning in her gut, tired of feeling out of her depth, tired of how this man had the power to tie her up in knots. She needed to end this now.

'Now take me to the airport—'

'You love me?'

Before she could blink he'd crushed her in his arms, a strange noise sounding suspiciously like a sob emanating from somewhere deep in his hard chest, pressed firmly against her.

For one, illicit moment she allowed herself to enjoy the feel of his strong arms holding her, to luxuriate in his familiar scent, to imprint this incredible feeling of being held by him to sustain her in the lonely months ahead.

However, as wonderful as the embrace was, it wasn't bringing her departure any closer, and she struggled out of his arms, gently pushing him away.

'It's irrelevant. Can't you see that?'

'Irrelevant? How can you say that?'

He reached for her again, and she stalled him by raising her hand.

'Because I know the truth. I know that whatever I feel would never be enough, when I know you don't feel the same way. You say you love me, but how can I trust you—after all that you've withheld from me, after all that's happened?'

Confusion clouded his proud features. 'But I have told you the truth now. Surely that makes a difference?'

Sighing, Bria swiped a tired hand across her eyes. 'It's hard for me. I grew up in an environment of mistrust where my dad constantly tried to buy my affection in order to interfere in my life, and my mum was so insincere I couldn't believe a word out of her mouth. Then when I escaped them I hooked up with a guy who only wanted me for my money. Then there's you…'

She trailed off, her heart twisting at the devastation creeping across his face that she'd placed him in the same tarnished package with her parents and Ellis.

'How can I trust you when everything that's happened since we first met, from you hiding your real identity to your motivation to be crowned king, has been hidden from me?'

A lump lodged in her throat and she swallowed, blinking back the tears that stung her eyes.

If she couldn't trust Sam, they had nothing.

'I can see my words are not enough.'

A perplexed frown appeared between his brows, doing little to detract from his dark good looks. 'But what about my actions? Did I not give you that book, knowing you would learn the truth? Am I not here? Did I not cancel a host of important meetings—the same meetings which would bring my grandfather's dream for Adhara to fruition—to convince the woman of my dreams to stay, to give us a chance?'

Bria opened her mouth to respond, but he placed a finger against her lips.

'You say my business is all important, that my country comes first. You are wrong, *habibati*. You come first. You are most important. You are everything to me.'

Bria might be many things—stubborn being one of them, according to Lou—but she wasn't stupid. And the passion blazing from Sam's eyes combined with the sincerity in his voice was enough to sow a tiny seed of doubt in her convictions.

'What does *habibati* mean?'

A silly question, considering the emotion of the moment, but she needed to buy some time to process what he'd just said, to absorb the fact that he was here with her—that he *had* run out on his precious business to stop her from leaving. Surely that meant something?

He captured her hand, his thumb caressing the palm in slow, concentric circles.

'It means "my beloved". For that's what you are—my beloved. My love. My only love. Now and for ever.'

Bria's breath caught as he raised her hand to his lips, brushing a gentle kiss on the back of it, holding it as if it were a priceless rarity.

'I have never felt this way about anyone. Only you. You are my one true love, my destiny.'

Her resistance wavered for a long, slow moment, before the first cracks in her defensive armour appeared.

'What about your business?'

'It will happen whether you agree to be my wife or not. I will see to it. I will also see to it that I never let it get in the way of my heart again.'

He picked up her other hand and brought it to his mouth, placing a longer, lingering kiss, this time on the palm.

Bria stifled a moan of pleasure, her body way ahead of her head in the forgiveness stakes.

'What about our differences?'

'What differences?'

He closed the short distance between them, slanting his lips across hers for a prolonged, exquisite moment.

'We are the same, *gummur*. Hiding behind business to mask past hurts, using success as a measure of who we are rather than taking a risk on who we can become if we take a chance on love, on each other.'

Any last, lingering doubts Bria had shattered as she flung herself into Sam's arms, smothering him, squeezing him, wishing she could crawl under his skin, just as he'd metaphorically crawled under hers.

'Does this mean you are willing to take a risk?'

Bria pulled back and stared into the face of the man she loved, the man who incredibly, unbelievably, loved her back.

'You bet,' she said, a coy smile curving her lips at the expression of joyful awe on Sam's face.

He loved her.

He truly loved her, and no matter what challenges they would face in the years ahead they would face them together. That was all that mattered.

'I love you, my beautiful Bria.'

Pure, indescribable joy filled her as she captured his face in her hands and leaned towards him. 'I love you too, Prince Sam.'

Bria felt his smile against her mouth as they sealed their union with a kiss that curled her toes, her fingers and sent white-hot heat shooting to all the places in between.

'You will marry me,' he whispered against the side of her mouth, drawing her into his arms and anchoring them firmly around her waist.

'Anyone ever tell you you're bossy and demanding?'

She pushed lightly at his chest, enjoying their banter, enjoying the thought of being Sam's wife more.

'I am the Prince.' He shrugged, his rueful grin at odds with the determined glint in his eyes.

'So what you say goes, right?'

'That is correct.'

Bria paused and tapped her lip with a finger, pretending to deliberate for a few moments, before letting out a whoop of joy.

'In that case, I'd better marry you. What do you think about that?'

He joined in her laughter, their new-found happiness knowing no bounds.

'I think we are going to lead a long and happy life together. It is written in the stars.'

'So you once told me,' she murmured, closing her eyes as he kissed her again, the sensual sweep of his lips against hers sending her to those stars he had so much faith in.

And she had no intention of coming back down to earth anytime soon.

MILLS & BOON PUBLISH EIGHT LARGE PRINT TITLES A MONTH. THESE ARE THE EIGHT TITLES FOR NOVEMBER 2008.

BOUGHT FOR REVENGE, BEDDED
FOR PLEASURE
Emma Darcy

FORBIDDEN: THE BILLIONAIRE'S
VIRGIN PRINCESS
Lucy Monroe

THE GREEK TYCOON'S CONVENIENT WIFE
Sharon Kendrick

THE MARCIANO LOVE-CHILD
Melanie Milburne

PARENTS IN TRAINING
Barbara McMahon

NEWLYWEDS OF CONVENIENCE
Jessica Hart

THE DESERT PRINCE'S PROPOSAL
Nicola Marsh

ADOPTED: OUTBACK BABY
Barbara Hannay

MILLS & BOON®
Pure reading pleasure™

1008 Rom LP

MILLS & BOON PUBLISH EIGHT LARGE PRINT TITLES A MONTH. THESE ARE THE EIGHT TITLES FOR DECEMBER 2008.

———————— ✄ ————————

HIRED: THE SHEIKH'S SECRETARY MISTRESS
Lucy Monroe

THE BILLIONAIRE'S BLACKMAILED BRIDE
Jacqueline Baird

THE SICILIAN'S INNOCENT MISTRESS
Carole Mortimer

THE SHEIKH'S DEFIANT BRIDE
Sandra Marton

WANTED: ROYAL WIFE AND MOTHER
Marion Lennox

THE BOSS'S UNCONVENTIONAL ASSISTANT
Jennie Adams

INHERITED: INSTANT FAMILY
Judy Christenberry

THE PRINCE'S SECRET BRIDE
Raye Morgan

1108 Rom